T0170979

Somehow He'd Ended Up with Someone Else's Coat

... and that act could end Robert Bowser's life
before it started.

His hand trembled as he answered the phone.

"Mr. Bowser?"

"Yes."

"Mr. Bowser, my name is Harvey Plangman."

"Yes, Mr. Plangman. I have your wallet, and jacket,
too, I believe."

"And I have yours."

"Why don't you drive over here? I could offer you
a drink and we could reclaim our things."

"Mr. Bowser, were you planning on going to
Brazil?"

Was this really how the world ended?

"You don't have anything to be afraid of,
Mr. Bowser."

"I'd better come there."

"Yes, I think it would be better if you came here.
You'll know who I am all right, Mr. Bowser.
I'm wearing your coat. . . ."

Intimate Victims

Vin Packer

Adams Media
New York London Toronto Sydney New Delhi

Adams Media
An Imprint of Simon & Schuster, Inc.
57 Littlefield Street
Avon, Massachusetts 02322

PROLOGUE BOOKS, ADAMS MEDIA and colophon are trademarks of Simon & Schuster, Inc.

The Simon & Schuster Speakers Bureau can bring authors to your live event. For more information or to book an event contact the Simon & Schuster Speakers Bureau at 1-866-248-3049 or visit our website at www.simonspeakers.com.

Manufactured in the United States of America

10 9 8 7 6 5 4 3 2 1

Library of Congress Cataloging-in-Publication Data has been applied for.

ISBN 978-1-4405-5610-4
ISBN 978-1-4405-3707-1 (ebook)

This work has been previously published in print format by:

Manor Books, Inc., New York, NY.

Intimate Victims

ONE

"AND HOW is Mother Franklin?" Wilford Clary asked.
"Oh, fine! Just fine!"

The truth, of course, was that Robert Bowser's mother-in-law was embarrassing and unbearable. He remembered last evening on the patio, before dinner. She had had her usual one-too-many cocktails. "During your conference tomorrow, Robert," she had cackled, "mention me to Wilfred Clary! You just tell him I'm still able to cut me a rug or two, and if *he's* nice to *you,* I'll be nice to *him!*"

Her tone of voice suggested several shades of meaning, and she wagged a sly, old wizened finger at Robert Bowser's nose. Since her seventy-seventh birthday, Margaret's mother seemed to go downhill in every direction. God knows her doctors' bills were bad enough—the rest was unbelievable. After decades of teetotaling, purse-lipped Victorianism, she had adopted a liking for gin and a coquettish personality. Along with this, an outdated slang and an unshakable conviction that she was "cute." Whenever Margaret and Robert entertained, Mother Franklin plunked herself down in the center of things, flirting with the men and warning the women that wine wasn't the only thing that aged well.

"A grand woman!" said Wilfred Clary. "A grand old woman!"

"Yes, indeed." Last year she had been $4,202 worth of grand old woman, in doctors' bills alone.

"Still enjoys a martini or two every evening?"

"Oh my, yes."

"Ha-ha! Yes, yes, a grand old woman! And Margaret's a grand young woman, Robert! You ought to be very thankful to have two grand women to watch out for you."

"Oh, I am," Robert said, thinking how glad he was that it was over now; he was free of them. It had been decided for him.

"Ha! Ha! Still enjoys a martini or two every evening! Ha-Haw! Well, well, I guess we're all settled with our business,

Robert." He took Robert's hand in a firm grasp. "It's up to *you* now. On your say-so, Cranston Biscuit Corporation will or will not become an acquisition of Baker Oats."

"Subject, of course," Robert said dully, "to approval by Cranston stockholders and to a favorable ruling by the Internal Revenue Service on the tax status of the transaction."

Those two things would stall matters—but only as far as Baker Oats was concerned. For Robert Bowser, the boil was finally at a head. He had already written Margaret a letter. It was in the jacket of the suit he was wearing—a full confession, along with a bland announcement that he was leaving the country and—it followed, didn't it?—leaving Margaret as well.

"Yes, yes, of course," Clary sighed. "Subject to all those conditions. You were always one for accuracy, Robert."

Not *this* time, Robert thought, and not that other time. Years ago there had been another slip, only dear Mother Franklin had come to the rescue. There was no chance of that happening again. Now that Margaret's mother was living with them, she would not even pay for her shoelaces. "Buy me an ice cream out of my will money," she would whine; or, "Who wants to take me to the movies with my will money?" Her favorite lead-in to conversation was: "When I'm dead and you two are rich as a result..."

Wilfred Clary said, "That's one reason I wanted *you* to have the directorship in Baker Oats. I trust your judgment in this matter, Robert. I know that in the past I've been rather cautious about trusting anyone's judgment but my own, but now...well, I'm getting old. There weren't all these mergers in my day."

"Yes, sir."

The old man eased into his leather swivel chair, in front of his time-blackened mahogany desk. The office was dominated by a huge safe to the right of his desk. The doors of the safe were black enamel, ornamented with a much-varnished landscape which was yellowed with age. In gold Spencerian script at the safe's top was lettered KING & CLARY, INVESTMENTS. King had been dead for years when Robert joined the firm. Most of the firm's business was concentrated on the investment of Wilfred Clary's money. King & Clary supplied financing for various companies which Wilfred Clary controlled in part. Acting as a silent partner, the investment company exercised a wide-ranging influence on those companies' management.

At forty-two, Robert Bowser was treasurer. His post had facilitated his embezzlement of $100,043.77 over a five-year period. Of that amount only $25,000 remained. Given a month or two, Robert could have quadrupled that sum, then doubled that in three months more, just as he had been juggling sums for the past five years—waiting for the coup that would make him both debt-free and rich. But it was all over now; the bubble had burst. He had miscalculated. Since King & Clary's original investment in Cranston (Robert had greatly exaggerated the amount, unbeknownst to either party, then had invested the difference at a good profit), Baker had seemed aloof from any suggestion of merger. Robert had a free hand with the manipulation of King & Clary's share of Cranston stock. There was no reason to anticipate a necessity for substantiation of recorded paper gains. It was impossible now to undo the damage in time to conceal the fraud. He had taken too many liberties with the account. If he were to keep his appointment in Winston-Salem on Tuesday, he would be found out before the day was over.

Clary was shuffling papers, and mumbling at his desk. Once Clary said a session was at an end, and they shook hands, Clary always insisted on reiterating everything for an additional ten or fifteen minutes.

Behind Clary's desk, on the ledge of the Southworth Building's twentieth floor, was a window washer. He was a man not much younger than Robert. There was a cigarette dangling from his lips, and he wore an old red-and-black checkered cap, the sort hunters wear. Pinned to his light blue work shirt was a huge round button. As he moved from one window to the next, while he slipped the safety belt to new notches, for an infinitesimal space of time the white belt whipped free at one end, dangled . . . an inch of risk before the man secured it.

Robert was fascinated. He moved closer to Clary's desk, so he could read the printing on the man's button.

". . . and they closed yesterday at 127¼, up 1⅛ for the day," Clary was murmuring to himself, "while Baker closed at 199⅛, down . . ."

Now Robert could see the words on the window-washer's button: KISS ME OR I'LL FALL FOR YOU.

Clary went on with the soliloquy of dry statistics. Robert felt as though he and Clary were figures in a dream, real only as long as the window washer watched them. If the window washer were to fall, even if he were to shut his eyes a second, Wilfred Clary's office would not exist. It was the window washer's world which was real, not Clary's and Robert's.

It was an idle, fuzzy daydream. If Robert had been concentrating seriously on his thoughts, it would be a familiar one as well. Many times during Robert Bowser's life it seemed as though nothing were happening to him, nor to the people he knew. Things were happening to people he read about in the newspapers or people he saw for a fraction of a second—here, there—faces in the crowd. A face distorted with anger—a face lit up with wild, uncontrolled laughter. A face of fear (he had seen a woman thrown to the street by a car, once, dragged a few feet—seen her eyes wild with fear). And once—he had never forgotten this face, the face of a man looking at a woman while they stood in a doorway on a New York street, late at night—the face of love. He never knew how he realized that it was love; he was sure that he had never seen it before, and certainly no one had ever looked at him that way, nor he at any woman that way—but he saw it, and he felt a strange give inside him, as if something were being taken out of him—and an emptiness.

Just for a few slow seconds then, while Clary kept on shuffling papers and mumbling, Robert closed his eyes. He had never tried doing that before, but he was not the same Robert Bowser, now that the boil was at a head.

With his eyes shut, he saw himself at a counter in a place that looked somewhat the way Robert had imagined Coney Island. There was a boardwalk like the one in Atlantic City. He stood at the counter and pointed to a rack of buttons. Someone beside him was playfully pushing his old hunting cap down over his eyes. The brim knocked the cigarette from between his lips, but in a quick, nimble flip of the wrist, Robert caught it between two fingers and popped it back in his mouth. He pinned the button on himself. People looked at him and grinned. He gave a smart, cocky salute back. Who was he with? A girl? Some friends? There was music playing, the corny kind heard at carnivals and skating rinks. He was very happy. It was so real!

Then he opened his eyes.

"The precise number of their shares outstanding," Clary

was saying, "will depend on the amount of their preferred stock converted and on the . . ."

Now Clary was putting papers into Robert's briefcase on the desk. It was the pigskin briefcase Margaret had bought him at Mark Cross for their twenty-first anniversary last month. He had given Margaret a gold bracelet from Cartier. He had more than his share of animal-skin briefcases, just as Margaret had safes full of jewelry. So it went, so it went.

Clary zipped up the briefcase and handed it to Robert.

Through the window, Robert could see just the legs of the window washer, who wore khaki pants and high-top shoes. The pants looked like old army issue. Robert had bought a pair for raking leaves, though he had a gardener and a lawn boy. During the war, Robert had worked at a desk in Washington. His eyesight was very poor; he wore huge glasses which gave him an owlish look, though without them he was handsome.

The laces of one of the window washer's shoes were bright red. A whim? Indifference? What? Again the white safety belt whipped in the air, dangled, was caught and locked. Risking so much for so little; why?

"I wish you a good trip, Robert. When will you reach Winston-Salem?" Clary asked.

"Monday afternoon."

"You're going by train, of course?"

He always did. It was safer. Suppose there were only a small chance a plane would crash; he had never taken *little* chances.

"Yes, by train." He would have to chance it now. Varig Airlines flew to Brazil; he had checked that.

"Good! Good! That will give you time to go over everything again before you see the Baker people Tuesday. You know, Robert," Clary removed his glasses as he did whenever he made a particularly personal remark, "I used to have Baker Oats for breakfast as a boy. I can still smell it cooking right there on the grate every cold winter morning . . . snow up to the window. I never thought I'd be part of them one day! Baker is a proud name, Robert. Cranston was bound to be swallowed up by someone. They couldn't do any better than Baker Oats! You'll be an asset to Baker too, Robert. Oh, I know all these years you may have thought I was holding you back, and maybe I was—maybe I was. But now I'm ready to give you the reins."

And if Wilfred Clary had said those words five years ago,

would it have made a difference? *All* the difference, Robert
Bowser believed. Three-quarters of Robert Bowser believed
it, anyway. The other quarter snickered to imagine the kind
of coup he might have accomplished, had he held the reins.
Billions, was all! Billions!

"Yes, sir," said Robert Bowser.

"You've done all right by Cranston, Robert. I think the
Baker people will see your handiwork after this meeting."

"Oh, I'm absolutely sure of that," Robert said. Quickly
he softened his assent to, "I mean, I *hope* so." He was
going to have to watch himself very closely—resist amusing
himself with subtle ironies, and continue to behave as
Robert Bowser had always behaved—modestly, compliantly
—for just a little while longer.

"Give my regards to Margaret and Mother Franklin, Robert. And have a good trip!"

"Yes, sir, thank you. Goodbye, Mr. Clary." *Goodbye for-
ever, Mr. Clary.*

They shook hands a second time. Robert looked back once
more at the window before he left the Southworth Building
for the last time. There was a blur of water obscuring the
pane, and for just an instant Robert felt a sudden terror of
the future—a sudden loss, as though the window washer had
in that instant slipped from the ledge. Then a hand reached
out and rubbed the water away, leaving the glass clear,
shining. The legs of the window washer appeared again
on the ledge. Robert felt a new spring to his step as he
went out of Clary's office.

II

"... but if you have a fourth drink before dinner, then so
will John Hark," Margaret was saying, "and we can kiss the
party goodbye."

The sky was pink; it was around seven p.m. The Lincoln
was clocking seventy, just outside Somerville, New Jersey.
They were on their way back to New Hope, Pennsylvania.
Margaret had driven into New York with Robert on the pretext that she had shopping to do. Robert knew the real
reason was that she could not wait to hear whether or
not Robert would get a directorship in Baker Oats.

With all the responsibility Clary allowed Robert to have,
he gave him very little in the way of title, prestige, or
financial reward. It was supposed to be enough, Robert

supposed, to be associated with King & Clary. It was not enough at all, and to compensate for this fact, Robert had made up little titles (director of this and that company) for Margaret's peace of mind. For his own peace of mind, there was the satisfaction that he was in an excellent position to reward himself as he saw fit, paying—so to speak—the director of this and that company out of the till. No other company for which Robert had worked had set him up so well for the coup. His present plight was his own fault, his own stupid miscalculation.

Margaret's pleasure with the directorship in Baker (his sixth, as far as she knew) was rooted in her belief that after all these directorships, Robert was now due to be King & Clary's next vice-president.

Beside him that evening in the Lincoln, she was already planning a dinner for their New Hope friends. It was planned for the day after Robert's return from Winston-Salem. No matter what sort of party she thought of having, John Hark's name invariably launched her on a long harangue about why he should not be asked. Hark was a drunk. To Margaret he symbolized waste of manpower, disorganization, nonconformity, and loss of control. All four, in whatever degree, made Margaret nervous and irritable. Robert had an idea that in some other way, too, John Hark reminded Margaret of Robert's own irresponsibility early in their marriage. That was Margaret's word for it—irresponsibility. It was Robert's other miscalculation. Robert had gambled $50,000 (a wedding present from Mother Franklin) into zero, on a highly speculative stock switch. The money was to have been for a new home, already under construction at the moment of disaster. Mother Franklin had stepped in and lent them enough to pay off the debt. Dutifully, Robert paid her back piecemeal, to the tune of $25,000. Then one Christmas, Mother Franklin wrote a note saying her gift that year was a cancellation of the remainder of the loan.

At the time, Robert was involved in another speculative project. With the help of some money "borrowed" from Brown & Forbes, his employers, and the $7000 he would have paid Mother Franklin against the loan, he played with some oil stocks until he eventually realized triple his investment. He then paid back Brown & Forbes and Mother Franklin. There was enough left to buy Margaret an emerald ring. Margaret was very proud of him, very relieved to see that he had learned his lesson and was applying himself so well at Brown & Forbes as to have received "a substantial bonus." Mother Franklin, never a fan of Robert's, was bravely disappointed. Her disappointment continued as Robert's success prevailed. A big chance here ... a big chance there ... and in between (sometimes two and three years went by without a gamble) Robert simply worked at what he was best at, manipulating money—for himself when he saw the opportunity, for his employers as a livelihood.

As they drove through Somerville, New Jersey, Robert only half-listened to Margaret's reasons for not inviting John Hark to *this* party. His plans for the future were so sketchy as to be practically nonexistent. He had never been to Brazil, and he spoke no Portuguese. He had only one contact in Brazil, a man named Bud Wilde, whom he had not seen for six years. Wilde ran a chain of laundromats in São Paulo. Robert knew very little more than that. This information had been scribbled across a Christmas card Robert had received last year from Wilde. There was the address and the telephone number, and a haphazard invitation to Robert to look Wilde up if he were ever down that way. Robert would look him up; beyond that, he could not carry his thoughts that evening.

For a moment, during the first part of their drive, he had pretended to himself that nothing had changed. He had told Margaret calmly about the trip he would have to take to Winston-Salem, about the directorship, and a few details of the merger plan. Then she talked and he listened. Listened, and predicted to himself that she would say just the sort of thing she did say. First, the new things they needed. A new car. A new freezer. All new solarium furniture. And—there was always one item he could *not* predict—a new tree for the west lawn. Then, the trip. The trip would come after the announcement that Robert was a vice-president. There was the Orient and there was Africa, or they could simply go to Nassau again. Right now, though, the party the day after Robert returned. Not a buffet again, no matter how many guests they invited. Margaret wanted a sit-down dinner. Robert became so caught up in his little game of pretense that he could see himself at the party. He was wearing his new light-tan shantung suit, crossing the lawn where Margaret needed a new tree, carrying a drink to someone. He was saying "Thank you" in response to someone's "Nice party, Robert." That had been his life, in a nutshell, for the past twenty-one years. Margaret said something, and he could see it in his mind's eye; then, before he knew it, the image had already come about, and he saw it on the screen of his memory.

". . . so if *he* comes," Margaret was saying now, "you just won't be able to have a fourth drink. Don't imagine you can sneak one without John Hark noticing it!"

There was that flat, emphatic note to her voice that told Robert she would take time out to reach into her bag for a cigarette. She never lit a cigarette when she was making a point, not Margaret. Margaret knew what she was about; Margaret had definite ideas. Robert turned his head away from the road and looked at her very carefully, taking her in with a certain wonder. He saw her in profile, the pale blue chiffon scarf whipping her cheeks in the wind, the creamy beige crêpe dress hugging her body; at the indentation of her bosom, the large gold necklace he had bought her at Jay Thorpe—her cool, soft features familiar, all of them —familiar as his own. Still, an enigmatic sensation filled Robert Bowser when he looked at his wife. He had been married to her for over two decades, yet he could predict only her performance, the same way he could predict the performance of an adding machine, or the Lincoln, or the sump pump at their house. In no way could he predict what Margaret was thinking, or whether she could stray as far from their lives as he so often did in his thoughts.

"There's a fifty-mile limit on this road," Margaret said then. "You're not nervous, are you? It's all over now, Robert."

"I wasn't nervous. You mean about the directorship?"

"Yes."

"I wasn't nervous about it."

"There's always a let-down after a build-up of anticipation. It's very common. You're probably a little depressed."

"Am I?" He wondered if that were true, that he was depressed. The truth was, he decided, he felt nothing.

"Very common," said Margaret. "A natural feeling."

"Do you have it ever?"

"Everyone does, of course. I just wish you'd slow down. You're driving too fast and we'll get a ticket."

Robert smiled to himself at her threatening him with the law.

Margaret said, "I don't blame you for driving fast through this part of the trip, though. I wonder how people live like this. I suppose they don't even know the difference. They're too caught up with basics—making a living, paying for the television set, raising children they can ill afford—basics. Slow down, please, Robert. Why don't we just exclude John Hark? We'll invite him another time."

It was a wretched landscape, full of paint-peeling diners and dilapidated houses built too close to the road; Tastee-Freeze stands, discount houses, oil drums for garbage, gas stations and billboards. There was a dump somewhere nearby, a stench from it, and smoke that hung over the area like a tired haze of hopelessness. Still, many, many times when Robert drove this route he felt not a repugnance like Margaret's, but a fascination—a wonder—and oddly, something akin to desire—not for any one thing, certainly not for *any one* —but for another way of being. There was a house along this route, somewhere very near where they were, a particular house that always happened to Robert. That was the only way he could think to put it. It "happened" to him. He was watching for it now.

"Do you want to exclude John Hark?" said Margaret.

"So I can have a fourth drink before dinner?" A fourth, he thought, and perhaps a fifth . . . and he saw himself in a small cafe in Brazil. It was hot and the cool drinks tasted marvellous.

"You'll feel a little festive when you return, Robert. Why shouldn't you have a fourth drink? Last week when all this Baker business came up, you were having four and five before dinner. One night I counted five."

"Were you worried?"

"Of course not! I've never once seen you intoxicated! You're not a John Hark. It's very simple."

"What is?"

"Don't be picky, Robert. You know what I'm saying. I can't tolerate drunkards, not John Hark's sort. He gets very sloppy, Robert. You *never* do! It's very simple."

"Yes, I guess it is. Very simple."

"Most things are," said Margaret. "We just won't ask him."

It was precisely then that Robert saw the house, at the very moment Margaret made it definite that John Hark was not to attend their party.

It was a run-down, squat, two-story house, gray shingle, next to one of Route 22's ubiquitous diners. The grass around it had not been cut in all the years Robert had been studying it. Many of the windows were broken. In front, the mailbox was damaged, so that the white container dangled off its post, upside down. In the side yard there was a rusty icebox, and on the front porch, bedsprings with a few coils popped. Perhaps this evening Robert noticed details he had not noticed before (he could not remember having seen the turned-over mailbox), but the house itself was the same and his feeling was the same. He knew the psychological name for his sensation was *déjà vu*—the feeling of having seen it before, and more—the feeling of hiving experienced it before. Lived in it? No, not that at all—experienced it was the only way he could think of it. Robert knew that the psychologists would point out that Robert had made the trip from Bucks County to New York and back countless times in the past fifteen years. He had probably seen the house, without thinking about it, for years, and only in recent years noticed it. Yet did that explain the sudden impact of shocking nostalgia that had overcome him the first time he had noticed it? And the same reaction, somewhat diluted by repetition, each time thereafter? The curious thing about it was that mixed with the nostalgia and the *déjà vu* was a sharp revulsion, a fear—a feeling that he had already experienced total degradation, and that the smell of it was in his nostrils and its taint all through him. At times he tried imagining himself living there, but he could not really visualize himself in the house. He could only wonder who would ever think to look *there* for Robert Bowser. It was before he had any reason to believe he would need a hideout. It was back in the years when he was in between risks, after he had left Brown & Forbes, and before he had become treasurer for King & Clary.

They drove beyond the house while Robert recalled those years. There had been opportunities, of course, and temptations. In Robert's work there always were. Robert's conceit was that he was selective and cautious—that he would not expend any energy on a project simply for the thrill of a gamble. Robert had a scorn for the petty gambler, the petty thief—the small mind whose ambition could be temporarily satiated by a lucky day at the racetrack or a successful venture through a bedroom window at night. The scorn was mixed with wonder as well—the same wonder Robert always felt when he observed people who had simply let go the rules, senselessly, flatly, and were facing the consequences. When he saw, in the tabloids, photographs of disheveled thugs who had been caught accosting their victims on city streets, in taxis, or hallways (usually with little more profit than ten or fifteen dollars), it was as though he were witness to their nakedness. He felt as though he had come across them walking around nude—a revulsion and a wonderment. What had ever made them think they could get away with it? In those years between risks, Robert asked himself that question often, and always with disgust for them, and for all get-rich-quickers. No, it took time and thought for the coup, and in the past five years, while Robert did not frame the thought exactly in his mind, part of his exhilaration was rooted in a dim awareness that he was not going for little things in a little way. No one would ever have reason—even now— to look in a house like that for Robert Bowser. That thought came to mind, and with it a strange inch of fear, and then Margaret's voice brought him back to the present.

"I said, shall we have dinner at the Canal House when we get to New Hope, or shall I fix something from the freezer?"

Robert Bowser took hold of himself, let the past moments all go ... even the near past and very pressing ones of his dilemma. He came full center to Right Now. Until Sunday night when the Varig jet left the ground, Right Now was the exigency. He must believe that and act in that belief. He was Margaret Bowser's husband. They were driving home and trying to decide, en route, where to eat.

He said, "I'd rather eat at Chez Odette, on the way into New Hope."

He even thought of escargots Bourguignons, saw the shells, smelled the pungent odor of the garlic sauce; saw his hands beside the plate, reaching for the silver implements for spearing and shell gripping.

The only trace of strain was the beginning of a severe headache. He could feel the pressure, as though somewhere in his brain was the minute start of a crack, prelude to a gradual crumbling, as though somewhere in the depths of his mind everything would come apart suddenly, if he could not contain the pressure.

TWO

HARVEY PLANGMAN was early.

He parked the MG in front of the Princeton Inn, in New Jersey, at quarter to six.

Lake Budde was not due for fifteen minutes. It had disappointed Harvey that Lake had not simply said, "Come on over to the house!"

Not only had it wounded Plangman's pride, it had also ruled out the possibility that Lake might invite him to stay overnight. Lake had made everything very clear.

"I have an hour to kill, I guess," he had said on the telephone. "I'll meet you for a drink."

Unless Harvey could work out something with Lois Cutler, it meant spending money for a motel. He had not planned to call Lois until tomorrow, but after several moments of nervous indecision, Harvey decided to make the call to Pennsylvania from here. It sounded good, too.

"Well, hi there, Lois," he would say, in a casual tone. "I'm over here in Princeton."

It would sound as though he were often driving about to places like that, doing this and that, looking up old friends and friends of the family, and sitting around on their grand old wide white porches, sipping something cool, looking out at a vast expanse of very green, long lawn.

When he walked inside the Inn, he saw the telephone booth immediately. He had always been very good at spotting telephone booths and men's rooms. It was a practiced accomplishment. He liked walking into a place and finding his way around without asking directions of anyone—just as though he were completely at home in his surroundings—as though he had been there many times.

This time, instead of going directly to the phone booth, he dallied by the front desk. He waited for the girl behind it to finish her conversation with an elderly gentleman. Harvey Plangman had decided that the girl had glanced up at him with a peculiar look as he walked in the door.

It was almost as though she were saying: What is *he* doing here?

Harvey was twenty-three years old, a native of Missouri, living now in Columbia, Missouri. He was very tall and thin, with jet black hair he wore in a combination ducktail-brushcut of his own invention. The white jacket he was wearing this evening was originally a waiter's. He had bought it at a uniform supply house, cut off the metal buttons, and sewed on white pearl buttons. It was a little something he had learned from the boys at Kappa Pi fraternity, where his mother was housemother. He wore the jacket's collar turned up in back, and turned up just slightly on the sides. He wore a light blue button-down shirt, a solid white tie, and in the center of the tie, a light blue stickpin. The stickpin had originally been a hat pin, which Harvey had bought in Woolworth's to match the shirt's color, then ingeniously filed down to size. The light blue handkerchief in the breast pocket of his jacket also matched the shirt's color, as did his socks. His dacron trousers were a near match, off-color just enough to blend in nicely. His shoes were white bucks. Harvey tried never to wear more than two colors at a time, and to tie in his accessories with the color scheme. He owned seven different kinds of watch bands, including an all-purpose scotch plaid one.

Harvey Plangman's father had died while his mother was seven months' pregnant. His mother had moved in with her mother in Columbia, Missouri, and Harvey was raised by the widows in a rickety, three-story yellow frame house on Wentwroth Street, in the heart of the state university section. As the years passed, the university expanded. Houses were torn down and replaced by bookstores, soda fountains, and haberdasheries. The widows turned down all offers for their house. They cooed over it and fussed with it, the same as they did with Harvey. It seemed neither the house nor Harvey would ever want, so long as the widows were their caretakers. After Harvey's grandmother passed away, the upkeep of the house and Harvey became too much for his mother. She accepted an offer from Kappa Pi fraternity to turn the house into an annex for them. Harvey slept on the couch in the living room, and his mother converted a side porch into her bedroom. The rest of the rooms were occupied by Kappa Pi's.

At first, this sudden masculine invasion fascinated Harvey. He hung about outside their rooms taking everything in with wide-eyed wonder. He noted the heavy, silver-backed hairbrushes, the shoe trees and shaving kits, and the aroma of tobacco, polished leather and costly brands of brilliantine. It was his first acquaintance with the paraphernalia of his own sex. He began to watch and tag after the frat brothers, to retrieve their nearly empty bottles of after-shave lotion from their wastebaskets, placing them on his own bureau, and to collect other things thrown out by them—worn leather wallets, shirts with frayed cuffs and collars, broken cigarette lighters—anything, everything.

There was an embarrassing moment one day when he picked a sweater off the banister, by the trash. There was a hole in the elbow, and spots down the front. He was under the impression it had been discarded by its owner, but that was a mistake. There was a fuss. Harvey returned the sweater, wanting desperately to explain that he had never intended to abscond with it, but the sullen-faced boy whose sweater it was, frightened Harvey into speechlessness. He handed over the sweater unsmiling and without a word.

There were other embarrassing moments. Once, when he was hanging about the third floor, sifting through the trash as silently as he could manage, a young bespectacled boy came from the room opposite, shouting like someone who had lost his senses. He was sick and tired, he declared, of Harvey sneaking around like a goddam Indian; sneaking around and pilfering.

Soon Harvey's mother received a typewritten, formal note from the proctor in charge of the annex:

It is absolutely essential that no one except members of Kappa Pi fraternity and their invited guests have access to the rooms and hallways which compose their living quarters. The only exception which can be be made is Maud Washington, cleaning woman!

After that, Harvey threw out every single thing of theirs which he had collected. In his fantasies he helped wizened old men across the street, and was the recipient of vast wealth upon their deaths the following day—a day which invariably ended with Harvey's brutal announcement to KP's annex proctor that the fraternity was to be off the premises by sunup.

After that too, Harvey developed a habit of taking things from stores in Columbia—not big things, not important things. He would carry a small razor blade wrapped in gauze in his jacket. Occasionally it would be a label that he would snip from a coat in one of the more expensive haberdasheries; sometimes, a set of handsome buttons from a sports jacket. Once or twice, he managed a tie, a pair of socks—little thefts. But he never took anything again from the Kappa Pi trash cans.

Evenings when Harvey and his mother were sitting down to dinner, a thunder of KP footsteps on the hall stairs would announce their mass departure. They were off to the House for their meal. It was, to Harvey's mind, very much like the return of the Royal Guard to Buckingham Palace. As they passed the living room doorway, some of them would glance in, wave, or simply gawk at Harvey and his mother, sitting at the card table they used for meals. Harvey always felt as though he were some strange, pathetic species which they had never before seen.

Sometimes, girl friends of the Kappa Pi's called on them at the annex. None of the girls Harvey knew were that pretty, or that sophisticated. There seemed to be some special aura of splendor about them, even those who were not pretty. There was a way about them; their hands seemed whiter and more graceful, and on their fingers they wore simply-cut gold rings containing a single pearl, or tiny, delicate little-finger bands with real diamonds dotted in arcs. Their hair seemed to shine; seemed softer, brighter, longer. When they spoke, they used their eyes with great self-assurance—an arch of the eyebrow, or a penetrating meeting of their eyes with yours, until you looked away uncertainly.

On occasion they would peer into the living room and say:

"Is *this* the Kappa Pi house? Is *this* 702 Wentwroth Street?"

Then to Harvey everything in the room would look, not just second-rate, but third- and fourth-rate. He wished his mother would stop wrapping the bottoms of flowerpots in aluminum foil. He wished they had window shades which were not torn and weather-stained. He wished, he wished— and outside in the hallway, some chuckling Kappa Pi would be telling a girl: "No, of course, *this* isn't the House. This is simply an emergency annex."

Chuckle, chuckle down the hall, a door slamming behind their Special Selves.

When the Kappa Pi house was finally completed three years later, Harvey's mother was asked to act as temporary housemother, until they could find someone else. In addition to room and board, his mother received a small salary. Some of it she shared with Harvey to keep their house running. With the rest, she began buying clothes. Harvey often saw his mother being escorted around Columbia by some shiny-faced Kappa Pi pledge. She was either being helped out of a taxicab in front of the local movie house, or being led up the steps of a local church on Sunday, a new hat perched on her head, a strange new smart way about her. Saturday afternoons he waved at her at football games, watched KP's place blankets across her lap, point out players and strategies to her—and weeknights she was often at the basketball games or track meets, with Kappa Pi boys proffering Cokes and hot dogs, running up and down the aisles to wait on her.

By spring, Harvey was conducting violent anti-fraternity sessions at the house on Wentwroth Street. He was leader of a small band of sour-faced boys who were filled with hard luck stories and liberal ideals. His mother had been asked to stay on permanently at Kappa Pi. Thanks to Kappa Pi, she told Harvey, Harvey could continue his education without her having to worry about him or the house on Wentwroth. More and more in their conversations, she compared Harvey to this one and that—to Farley or Lake or Tub or Blaise. None of them had names like Harvey, it seemed. None of them had names like Earl, Edgar, Harold or Leroy. The boys with names like that were dropping ashes all over Harvey's living room, leaving Harvey's kitchen strewn with dirty glasses and empty beer bottles, and agreeing with Harvey that well-groomed, polite, orderly Kappa Pi's and their like should be abolished. Eventually, Harvey threw them all out and went a solitary way. Some evenings he would call on his mother at the House. It was a huge mansion, built in the grand Southern style, with eight great white columns in front, a vast row of red brick steps, a horseshoe-shaped drive, and a uniformed colored cook, along with two aged Negroes who wore white coats and bowed all the time, and who the KP's called "houseboys."

Harvey's mother was always asking him what his plans were. He was enrolled in a course of general studies at the university. His mother said that he ought to be pre-something. The fraternity men were nearly all pre-something. Pre-med, pre-law, pre, pre, until Harvey would get so angry with her that he would shout at the top of his lungs. Then, always, came the rapping at the door, the solicitous voice:

"Are you all right, Mom Plangman?"

Outside, as Harvey whipped by and into the night, was an anxious, apple-faced Little Lord Fauntleroy, with his diamond pin fastened to his cashmere sweater.

Harvey did not even know what he wanted to be, and he spent as much time puzzling over that, as he did wondering about KP's like Case Bolton, for example, who had simply decided to be a corporation lawyer. How did someone simply decide to be that?

All Harvey knew was that he wanted Things.

Once when Tub Oakley had said, "What things?", Harvey could not answer with one of Tub's smooth, quick, specifics.

He had answered, "A car."

"What kind?" Tub wanted to know.

A big one, was all Harvey could think. He did not answer Tub. He knew the KP's liked to show him up— Things, he wanted. Big things!

From a Columbia stationery store, Harvey stole a genuine leather notebook, in which he recorded the names of things, copied from magazines. In his wallet too, he kept lists of things, along with a vocabulary list he was memorizing.

At Kappa Pi, Harvey was always treated with a great show of cordiality. He was often invited for meals, sitting beside his mother at the front table. In this new phase of Lists Of Things, his fantasies were of Tucker Wolfe or Boy Ames, or some other dignitary of Kappa Pi, taking him aside, arm around his shoulder, voice confidential, warm, saying solemnly: "Harv, the more we've known you, the better we've liked you! We want you to be one of us!"

He watched their coming and going with despair and desire, going through half a dozen more phases. In one, he took a lover, a woman twenty years older than he was. Gertrude taught shorthand at a business school in Columbia. She had been married and divorced, and Wednesday evenings without fail, she attended the local meetings of Alcoholics Anonymous, where she spoke too, on occasion. She wore a pure white streak down her dyed black hair, off-the-shoulder blouses and peasant skirts, and always something from Mexico, where she had once spent two years.

Harvey moved her right into the house on Wentwroth Street, though Gertrude maintained her own apartment for appearances. He did not love her in the least, but he loved the way he thought it looked—that he was under the spell of a mysterious older woman, who had been a drunk at one time, and had lived in Toluca de Lerdo. He bought her bright scarves and drank beer with her in the student haunts around Columbia, and sometimes he walked her by the Kappa Pi house, pretending he was too absorbed in what they were saying to one another to wave at the boys on the front porch.

He was relieved when his mother finally insisted that Gertrude was to stay out of the house on Wentwroth. He had grown weary of her incessant chain smoking and Coke drinking, and of her dogged insistence on receiving her satisfaction during the long sessions of love-making required to accomplish this.

Ultimately he dropped out of school because he was failing his subjects. He entered an easy money phase, dreaming of scheme after scheme for making a small fortune overnight. He became a bootlegger for students who were tired of drinking beer in "dry" Columbia, supplying them with whisky he bought in Jefferson City. His profits from this enterprise were considerable, until his customers noticed the whisky was weak-tasting, the seals on the bottles tampered with. He got rid of the remainder of his watered-down stock at drunken frat brawls, where he would show up near the end, when the supply was diminishing. Then he abandoned that business for a part ownership in a Hoagie-Pizza stand. His partner was not nearly so forgive-and-forget as the customers for his whisky. He was forced to make up the shortage in profits, when it was discovered, and forced to sell his half at a loss. There were other ventures, each one a worse failure than the last; each one involving more loss of face.

His mother was still in Enemy Camp, and the Kappa Pi's were still superior. He accepted this finally, as a fact. The frustration that accompanied it filled him with a longing for a way around the fact. Until he met Lois Cutler, his only resort was to imitate and hate the Kappa Pi's, to collect their injustices and to love them.

The night Harvey met Lois Cutler, he had just happened to wander over to the Kappa Pi house to visit his mother. He had just happened to wear evening clothes (rented), on the pretext that he was dropping in on the graduation dance at the University gym. The campus was busy with all sorts of dances; it was the last night of school. Harvey feigned great surprise at the elaborate festivities he found underway at Kappa Pi. Elbowing his way through the couples dancing to the twelve-piece orchestra, he went directly to his mother's suite on the first floor. He knew she would not be there, that she was undoubtedly hovering over the punch bowl in the main room, or making the wallflowers feel wanted, but he assumed an important air as he headed for her suite—an "all-business" attitude. He intended to sit in her parlor and smoke a cigarette, then slowly, unobtrusively, blend with the crowd. When he came upon his mother, he intended to say, with a certain pique in his tone: "I've been looking all over for you!"

He was surprised to find his mother's suite occupied. The occupant was talking on the telephone in his mother's bedroom. Harvey sat down on the couch in the parlor and lit a cigarette.

"All right, Daddy, I promise," a girl's voice was saying. "I cross my heart . . . What? No, he didn't try to get *me* drunk. No, Daddy. I told you, he flunked geology and he felt bad because he won't graduate."

The girl was talking about Tub Oakley, Harvey knew. He guessed she was a Stephens College girl. Tub always dated Stephens girls. They usually had money, for one thing; for another, it was not easy for Tub to get a date with acceptable sorority girls. He was too fat and too short. Stephens girls usually dated Tub to get to fraternity parties where they could meet more men. Stephens was not co-educational.

"Daddy," the girl said, "I told you I never went out with him before! How was I to know he'd get so drunk! No, I promise. I cross my heart and hope to die . . . What? . . . I don't want *you* to die either, Daddy . . . What? . . . No. I promise I won't go home with him. I'll take a taxi. Hmm? . . . Now? Long-distance?"

The next thing Harvey knew, the girl was singing in a high little squeaky voice.

"Daddy, I want a diamond ring, big cars, everything,
Daddy, you've got to get the best for me, eee,eee,eee,
Oh, Daddy, you've got to get the best for meeeeeeeee."

Then the girl giggled for a few seconds... "I miss you too. Hmmm? Oh, a mile's worth... All right, a trillion, million miles worth. Don't worry. I cross my heart, Daddy."

Harvey was beginning to feel uncomfortable and curious. He leaned forward and peered around the corner of the parlor slowly. The girl's back was to him. She was sitting on his mother's bed, the phone cradled in her arms, her head bent to her shoulder, squeezing the phone's neck in place. Her hands were caressing her arms. She had long yellow hair which spilled down a very white, bare back. She was wearing a lemon-colored net gown, ankle-length, and high-heeled gold slippers.

"Here's a kiss," she said. She made a smacking noise with her lips.

Harvey leaned back. He heard her say, "See you tomorrow night, Daddy. God bless me and God bless you, keep each one and keep us two... I will, Daddy... I won't, Daddy. I promise. Bye-bye!"

She jumped when she came out of the bedroom and saw him sitting there.

Harvey stood up and bowed. He introduced himself. He apologized for being unable to help overhearing her telephone conversation. Then he offered to see that she got home all right. She accepted this offer, along with Harvey's offer of a soda en route. Harvey escorted her from the Kappa Pi house with a sense of deep satisfaction. If there was any Kappa Pi he hated more than all the rest, it was Tub Oakley. If there was any Kappa Pi he longed to show up above all the others, Oakley was that Kappa Pi.

"Shouldn't I try to find Tub and tell him I'm going home with you?" Lois Cutler asked.

"He's probably upstairs getting sick," said Harvey. "Anyway, he doesn't deserve any courtesy. Never mind his excuses, it was very bad form."

"That's what Daddy says."

"Did you call him long distance just to ask what to do?"

"I always consult Daddy."

"Are you from Kansas City or St. Louis?"

"Pennsylvania," she said. In his mind, Harvey was adding up the minutes—estimating the phone call's cost.

"Daddy and I are extremely close," Lois Cutler said.

"So it seems."

"He's such an old silly," she said.

"That's very nice," Harvey told her.

He looked down at her. She was not a very pretty girl. Her eyes were a trifle too close together, and her lips were as straight as a boy's. Her hair was really golden, though, and she had very bright green eyes, that were now lit with high pleasure. "A silly old silly," she purred, "and I *loves* him!"

Instead of the soda, they went for beers to one of Columbia's tawdry cafes, on the fringes of the university campus. She had just been graduated from Stephens, and she was eager to return to Pennsylvania—to Daddy. She was unable to concentrate for very long on any subject besides Daddy. Around her neck, a tiny gold locket contained a picutre of Hayden Cutler. From her jeweled brocade clutch bag, she produced another, a larger one which showed him full-length, leaning against a white Citroen DS 19. (Harvey had no trouble identifying the car; it had been on one of his April lists.) Daddy was a dapper, laughing gentleman, with a thick head of white hair and a beefy youthfulness.

"Isn't he cute?" Lois wanted to know.

"He's a very nice looking man."

"Him works too hard," Lois said to the photograph, pouting and slapping it with her finger. "Him works his fingers to the bone!"

"What sort of work does he do?"

"He has a seat on the New York Stock Exchange," Lois said. "Him's a biggy old Wall Street daddy doll."

Harvey found that he was not bored or even repelled by the subject of "Daddy," even though he was beginning to suspect that Tub Oakley's geology grades might not have been the sole reason he had gotten drunk. Harvey had never seen anyone of Lois Cutler's type in such a vulnerable position, unless she were intoxicated. At first, he listened to her palaver about Daddy with the excited feeling that at any moment she would realize she had been talking about nothing else. He expected that then she would be embarrassed and apologetic, and attribute her uninhibited confidences to the

fact that Harvey made her feel unselfconscious. When he
realized no such thing was going to happen, he took a new
tack. He began extolling her utter devotion to "Daddy," hop-
ing to shame her into some sort of awareness of the fact
she was the next thing to neurotic about her father. He
expected her to say during a pause, which he tried desperately to effect: "I guess you think I'm crazy or something."
But there were no pauses. The subject of Daddy was an
inexhaustible reservoir. Unable to fight it, Harvey joined it.
He found himself not only interested in Daddy, but vaguely
delighted by the unabashed Lois, who poured out her feelings to him, and whose hands were whiter, whose hair was
longer and more shining than any other girl Harvey had
known—and whose penetrating eyes Harvey found himself
looking into without flinching.

When Harvey and Lois reached the dormitory at Stephens
late that evening, small knots of other couples stood under
the eaves embracing. While Harvey was deciding whether or
not to kiss her, she pulled him under the porch light.

"I'm going to do something I've never done before," she
said.

He felt like kissing her, but he wondered how such small
lips would feel. He did not think it would be much of a kiss.

"What's that?" he said. He wanted to guide her back from
the light a bit, but when he stepped back, she pulled his
sleeve again.

"No, stay right there." Then she fumbled in her clutch
bag until she came up with a wrinkled piece of paper.
"I'm going to show you something."

She was not going to kiss him after all.

"It's the beer," she said. "I've never shown this to anyone before. That old silly wrote it."

"Your father?"

"Himself!" she giggled.

"It's a poem."

"Well, let me see it."

"First I want to tell you that he's such a silly old silly.
He scribbled it on a menu at 21 in New York City. He
took me there before I left for school last fall. We had
frogs' legs and wine, and wine, and wine. It's his silly old
wine poem."

"They'll be calling curfew any minute, Lois."

Behind them, a thin boy with intense eyes was comforting a weeping blond with the promise that he would tell Kathy the truth about them, the moment he arrived home.

"Just remember it's a silly old daddy wine poem," Lois said. Daddy said I should show it to every boy I go out with. But I never have. For reasons that will become obvious when you cast your eyes upon old silly's silly."

She handed it to him, and pressed her fingers to her lips, giggling again. "I copied it off the menu and typed it up," she said.

FOR BOYS WHO KNOW LOIS

by a man who knows her better!

Lois is a lady, have no doubt at all,
Presented to Society at New York's Gotham ball,
The New York Junior Assembly counts her as a member,
Her maternal grandparents were Bea and William Kemper,
Descended from John Alden, and Henry Adams too,
Her uncle is a Boocock, affectionately called "Boo."
The Cutlers came from Devonshire in 1636,
They excel in everything, industry, politics.
Bear in mind the facts, my boy, regard the family tree,
If you want no more, even, than just to be her caddie;
If you're not a gentleman, you'll answer to her daddy!

"Isn't that an old silly, though?"
"Can I write you?" said Harvey Plangman.

All of that was two months ago.

Between then and now Harvey had spent his time managing Woolworth's five-and-ten, pocketing a good quarter of the inventory, and corresponding daily with Lois Cutler. He fantasized their honeymoon visit to his mother, the Citroen DS 19 they had borrowed for the cross-country trip parked outside the Kappa Pi house. Even Tub Oakley (who was in summer school trying to pass geology) was impressed by the volume of mail that came from Lois to the Kappa Pi house, addressed to Harvey. Harvey had not bothered to mention the fact he was neither a university student, nor a Kappa Pi. He had borrowed a set of maternal and paternal grandparents from the wedding announcements in *The New*

York Times, and he had killed off his father, a colonel, in World War II. His letters to Lois were as filled with "embellishments" as hers with references to Daddy. As the weeks wore on, a change came over Harvey Plangman. The more he lied, the more he wished his lies were true. He began to brood over the unfairness of the fact they were not true. He began to feel protective toward his lies, almost as though they were little living creatures whose existence depended on him. He became slightly reticent and suspicious, and in the fantasy of his honeymoon visit—to his mother, he was always compelled to go out on the steps of the KP house and shout, "All right, boys, please get away from the car!"

Another facet of this change was the thought that certain people were on to him—here and there he would run across one of them. They looked at him in a peculiar way.

That cool July evening, at the Princeton Inn, where he was meeting Lake Budde, it was the girl at the desk.

While he waited for her to finish her conversation, his eyes fell to a small basket of matchbooks set out on the counter, each one with PRINCETON INN marked on the cover. Harvey Plangman prided himself on never pocketing a place's matchbooks, never once giving a place the satisfaction of thinking that he would like to show off their matchbooks. Instead, for a dollar, Harvey sent away periodically for 30 matchbooks from famous hotels and niteries. He sent his dollar to a P.O. box in New Orleans, copied from an advertisement in the *St. Louis Post Dispatch*. That way, he not only had matchbooks from places he would probably never visit, he also saved face by never being seen in the act of picking up one for a keepsake. Yet, anyone who knew Harvey Plangman at all, knew he was never without a matchbook from a famous hotel or restaurant.

Harvey edged over closer to the girl behind the counter, as the gentleman she was talking with moved away.

"Yes?" she said.

"I beg your pardon," said Harvey, bowing, "would you be good enough to inform me of the location of your telephone booth?"

She pointed to it. "Right over there."

"Thank you *most* kindly."

"You're welcome."

She was looking down at his hands. He realized he had been standing there cracking his knuckles. He dropped his hands to his sides. Then he said, "Oh, by the by," with a casual air, "one other thing."

"Yes?"

"Would you be good enough to tell me where I might purchase a copy of *Fortune* magazine?"

"We don't sell magazines."

"Oh, I'm aware of *that!* I simply thought you might know where I could purchase *Fortune.*"

"I don't know."

"Oh, dear!" said Harvey. He sighed. "It's quite important that I obtain it. Something pertaining to business."

"Umm hmm."

"Well, thank you anyway. I'll find it someplace!" he said importantly.

The girl seemed unimpressed. She licked her finger and began shuffling papers.

Harvey took out his new cigarette case, removed a Player's cigarette (he had switched brands last week, from Virginia Rounds to Players) and reached for a pack of the Princeton Inn matches. He lit the cigarette, blew out the match, and left the matchbook on the counter in front of the girl. Then he walked back slowly, inhaling nicely, to make his phone call.

THREE

ON THE way to Lambertville Margaret said, "and I think for this party I'll go back to round butter balls again. They always look more formal, somehow. I don't mean formal exactly, but you know what I mean, Robert. We always used to have round butter balls before the war, remember?"

"Umm hmm," said Robert. He was thinking that he would probably miss Margaret; it would probably hit him all of a sudden, once he got to Brazil. After all, he had been with Margaret for twenty-one years. He would *have* to miss her, wouldn't he?"

"I haven't seen round butter balls in years, now that I think of it," said Margaret. "No, I really don't think I have."

"Margaret," Robert said, so impulsively that he was surprised at the sound of his own voice, "I love you." He simply wanted to test the sound of those words again; did they have *any* meaning? The instant they were out, he realized they did not. He loved no one.

"Why do you suddenly announce it?" said Margaret.

"Maybe it's your perfume. What is it?"

"Balenciaga's Quadrille? I wear Quadrille most of the time."

He glanced at her to see if she were pleased. Her eyes looked back unsmiling, concerned. He wondered if Margaret ever had the feeling she could not contain pressure in *her* head. He wondered, if he were to tell her that he had that feeling now, what she would say. *"How can you sit there with the feeling you can't contain pressure in your head, saying you love me, Robert?"*

"Oh, well, it's an innocent remark, isn't it?" said Robert.

"I'm just interested in why you made it at that particular moment."

"I guess there wasn't any reason."

"Well, what promoted it? Did it come out of the blue?"

"Out of the blue," said Robert.

"You must know what prompted it. Go back over it. I

33

was saying that I hadn't seen round butter balls for years.
That's just what I was saying when you said it."

"Said what?" Robert felt uncomfortable and silly now; he
knew she would not drop the matter, and he hated that.

"You know what. What you just said."

"Is it so hard for *you* to say the words?" He was tired
of his own voice bantering with her, but he could not stop
this asinine conversation.

"Robert, you're acting very strangely today. I know you've
been under a tremendous strain over the Baker thing,
but. . ." and he hoped she too was tired now, of the whole
thing. She let her sentence go unfinished, sucked on her
cigarette, and stared out the window moodily.

He gave her knee a gentle squeeze and said, "I'm sorry,
Margaret. I must be a bore. I probably am a little nervous,
you're right."

"That's all right, dear." She glanced across and smiled at
him.

He smiled back. "We'll have a nice meal at Chez Odette."

"I do wish, though, that you could explain why you
made that remark just at that time, Robert. Did round butter
balls remind you of something in our past?"

No, he was not going to miss Margaret. He forced himself
to say calmly, pleasantly, "I honestly don't know, Margaret.
As you say, it came out of the blue. Will you please accept
that answer? Will you cross it off to strain, nerves, tension—
anything?"

"Have it your own way!" Margaret snapped.

He laughed bitterly to himself at the idea of Margaret
allowing him to have his own way. It was a safe, meaningless offer, and Margaret knew it. Perhaps she had sensed
that about him when she had married him, in the same way
he had sensed (but never said it out to himself) the fact that
if Margaret had not had money, he might not have loved
her. It was not the dollars and cents aspect of Margaret's
money—but all that someone like Margaret represented to
Robert: prestige, refinement, security. All those things Robert himself possessed, in a lesser degree. If Robert's father
had not gambled away the family fortune, things might have
been different—but worse than any poor boy's awe of a
rich girl, was a once-rich boy's hungry nostalgia for the past.
Worse than fear of being poor, was the fear of not being
rich.

When Robert had courted Margaret, he had thought of it

as a big gamble, with the odds quite a bit against his win-
ning her. He had attributed his success to his skill at the
game. He had been far too young and ingenuous to appreciate the fact there had to be something in it for Margaret
as well, an intangible something that had nothing to do with
Robert, but with Margaret's determination to have her own
way.

He had read somewhere that people deserved each other,
particularly husbands and wives. The fishwife deserved her
husband's beatings and the Milquetoast deserved his wife's
nagging—not only deserved it, but was pulled toward it, like
a hairpin to a magnet.

He could remember the years and years of giving in to
Margaret, and all the accouterments of the process—the
hot water bottles, the long distance calls to Mother Franklin, the thermometers and bottles of nerve medicine, and
Margaret's martyred silences—until Robert said, "If you
really think we ought to . . ." or, "If you really think we
shouldn't . . ." It was a pattern, he knew, dating back to his
youth; his life had always been controlled by someone
with a stronger will than his. Margaret's sick headaches and
sorry expressions were not unfamiliar, which was one reason Margaret and Robert's mother had been arch enemies
from the moment they met, until Mrs. Bowser's demise. Yes,
the pattern was as clearly marked as a tire tread in fresh
snow. It was not simply Margaret's money which had drawn
Robert to her; nothing was ever that simple. Robert Bowser
had learned that slowly and very well. With every gamble,
there was a more subtle gratification involved than just win-
ning the prize.

He glanced over at his wife, who was silent now, peeved.
She pretended to sleep. Her left leg swung nervously on
her right one. Robert knew how Margaret hated unpredicta-
bility, and how much she believed that there was an answer
to everything. She was probably right now searching for the
very sentence she had said *before* the one about round butter balls—searching for some clue to the mystery of his
sudden declaration of love. A part of him wished it had
been another way. "I love you, Margaret," he would have
said, because he would have felt very close to her after
twenty-one years of marriage—close, and not at all self-
conscious about expressing his affection. And Margaret
would have reached across and touched some part of him,
smiling. She would have said, "I love you too, darling, very

much." But then, they would have had to be two different people.

He could not honestly say life with Margaret had been unpleasant. Her control was consistently benevolent; firm, but very gentle. She had a way of leading him to believe that she knew him much better than he knew himself; that she was just a little surprised he did not know himself that well. His mother had known the same tricks. "Robert," she used to say, "you don't *really* want to do that?" Whatever it was he had wanted to do, he put it out of his thoughts— and gladly. That was the peculiar part. It seemed almost as though he asked to do certain things, simply to please her by then not doing them.

A year after he had been married to Margaret, they had gone to Paris. They had stayed at a small hotel on the Quai des Grands-Augustins, in a suite on the top floor, with a balcony that looked down on the Seine and the Ile de la Cité. The wine and the contagious notion of Paris' pull toward the romantic, the fact they were alone together in a foreign country, and the pleasure in buying Margaret a jewel from Christofle—a whole gentle mood of desire and delight —had inspired Robert during love-making. He had felt nearly spiritual as he touched her body; there was a new dimension to their intercourse which thrilled him. Then, in the middle, Margaret stopped him.

"The traffic noise," she said. "I'm sorry, Robert. I just can't concentrate."

He remembered that he had not been as disappointed by Margaret's failure to feel a difference as he had been struck by the idea of Margaret's concentrating on something then. On what? It had never occurred to him that she concentrated when they made love. He had put his pajamas on and smoked a cigarette by the window a while; then he had asked her what it was she concentrated on during lovemaking.

She had answered, "That isn't like you, Robert."

Immediately Robert had felt immense relief. The feeling had surprised him, but there it was—and he had mumbled that he was only kidding.

Another thing that Margaret felt was not at all like Robert, was Robert's friendship with Bud Wilde. Wilde had been Robert's roommate at Princeton, and the year Robert was graduated, Wilde was his Best Man. Friendship was a slight exaggeration. Necessity had forced them on one an-

other. Wilde had taken the initiative in making the best
of it. Robert was reserved and bespectacled, solemn and already engaged to Margaret. Wilde called him "Stuffy" and
treated him with that combination of affection and tolerance
that sometimes happens between opposites when intimacy is
thrust upon them. They were somewhere on the outskirts
of friendship, and for Robert, it was the closest he had ever
come. Wilde, the younger of the two, treated Robert good-
naturedly, as one would treat a kid brother who had turned
out to be a disappointment, but was still kin. At Robert's
wedding, Wilde got very drunk and told the entire wedding
party an obscene joke that had to do with a honeymoon
night and a busy hotel elevator. After that, he was Margaret's favorite target, until years later when John Hark came
into their lives.

Robert had seen Wilde several times during the war years,
when Bud passed through Washington. Bud was a Navy pilot
with Task Force 58, in the Tokyo area, Iwo Jima, Jyushu,
and the islands of Nansei Shoto. Before the war was over,
he had flown twenty-six missions. Whenever they lunched
or drank together, it was Wilde who talked, while Robert
sat dumbly, fighting an inevitable headache, and a fear there
would be a lapse in the conversation, when he would have
to think up something to say.

Once Robert had blurted out, "How I envy you!"

It was only half true. Part of Robert Bowser did envy
Wilde, but the rest, the greater part of him, saw Wilde's
ostensible intrepidity as foolishness; risks too great for the
gain.

"Then do something about it, Stuffy, before you're fat and
forty!"

"I tried to get in . . . My eyes are . . ."

"I'm not talking about the war, Stuffy," Wilde said.
Neither was Robert talking about the war. He was talking
about Bud himself, about caution thrown to the wind, and
little gambles—about impetuosity and the thread of daring
woven through Robert Bowser's own cloth. Robert was always given to wonder what it would be like if there were
more there. He let Bud go on, without telling him his
thoughts.

"You're like one of those spiders that walks on top the
water all the time," said Bud. "Get wet, Stuffy! Listen—have
you ever done anything just on impulse? You know what
I mean, taken a foolish chance, hopped in the sack just for

a good hard kick, ever done anything totally unthought-out, just because you goddam felt like it?"

"Margaret's perfectly adequate in bed," Robert had answered, knowing how dull it sounded, but thinking that he could not tell Wilde the idea just seemed unnecessary. Was that it? Or was it that he simply knew people didn't get away with things? You couldn't get away with it, and Wilde didn't know it.

"Stuffy," Wilde went on, "a kick—a real kick, is never described by the adjective 'adequate.' Neither is a real risk, nor an impulse. What you need to do, Stuffy, is to take off your goddam gloves!"

"Yes," Robert had sighed, "I remember that poem."

All the while they had roomed together, Bud had a poem tacked to his mirror. Robert forgot who the poet was, but he could still see the small index card with the poem typed on it, the red thumbtack holding it.

TO A FAT LADY SEEN FROM THE TRAIN

O why do you walk through the fields in gloves
Missing so much and so much?
O fat white lady whom nobody loves,
Why do you walk through the fields in gloves,
When the grass is as soft as the breast of doves,
And shivering sweet to the touch?

Robert had resisted the notion of telling Bud about the $50,000 gift from Mother Franklin, which he had lost on the stock deal. It would have astonished Bud, but Robert did not want to put it down as a risk taken and lost. A miscalculation, not a gamble. Wilde would not understand that— that there was a difference. It was the difference between big business and little business, between the graceful maneuverings of heads of industry and the paltry caviling of street peddlers.

Wilde had sighed. "It was tough that Margaret roped you in so early, Stuffy."

"I wanted to marry Margaret very badly," Robert answered honestly.

Bud Wilde had smiled. "Who was it who said that when the gods want to punish us, they answer our prayers?"

The last time Robert saw Bud Wilde was the same day Robert was made treasurer of King & Clary.

It was a day in March. He had not seen Bud in fifteen
years. Clary had ordered a standby that day. It meant Robert was to keep himself available at a moment's notice for
a call to the twentieth floor. There was the usual electricity
in the air; the cluster of secretaries and file clerks whispering by
their desks the elevator boy holding the special elevator for
the express trip to twenty; the hush of tension, and the leap
of temporary relief at the phone's every ring.

Bud had called New Hope and Margaret had told him
where Robert worked. Impulsively, wanting to surprise Robert, Bud had gone directly to the Southworth Building without calling.

Their reunion took place one minute after Robert had
received word he was due on twenty. Wilfred Clary was a
stickler for punctuality, and for all the petty ritual and protocol of the patriarchal company life. Robert was actually
running down the hall toward the elevator. There, in the
corridor between his office and the elevator, he came upon
Wilde. For a moment he did not recognize him. His first impression was that Bud Wilde was one of the brash Coronet
cigar salesmen, since Coronet Corporation had offices on
eight too. When Wilde slapped him across the back, pulling Robert's coat sleeve at the same time, Robert had
stepped back, the beginnings of a reproachful look spread-
ing across his face—then slowly changing as Bud called out,
"It's me, Stuffy! Bud!"

He was dressed in a seedy tweed suit, a blue shirt, and a
loud blue and red tie. Brown shoes. A worn felt hat in his
hands, with weather stains on the band.

"It's Bud!" he grinned, pounding Robert's shoulder.

"Hello!"

"Hel-lo? Holy Christ, is *that* all?"

Then had come the embarrassment of trying to explain
to Wilde that he was due on twenty immediately. There
was Wilde's disbelief: immediately meant immediately, not
two minutes, not five. Robert was perspiring, beads of it
dotted his forehead and he could feel his shirt sticking to
his ribs. Wilde sensed the seriousness of Robert's situation
slowly, perhaps not until Robert was walking away—perhaps not until the elevator doors had sealed off Robert from
view, leaving Wilde there with his bewilderment. They had
arranged for a drink at the Roosevelt at five-thirty. All the
way up to twenty, Robert Bowser thought of Wilde's last
words in the corridor, "Why, Stuffy, you're about to pee in

your pants—like some kid on his way to the principal's office!"

When they met later in the Rough Rider Room, Bud told Robert he had been doing some test-piloting, some stunt-flying at state fairs in old World War I crates, and some freight piloting between the States and Brazil. Robert had just been told of his appointment as treasurer. In the back of his mind, Robert Bowser knew what the new position meant to him: a chance at the coup. He could not frame it right out, but he knew that as he listened to Bud and his talk of wild schemes for the future, he felt vaguely resentful and impatient with Bud. Things took time; things had to be thought out—timing was everything—*everything*. It was almost as though he feared some of Wilde's reckless impulsiveness would rub off on him, if he were to listen to Wilde any longer. There was just enough of Wilde in Robert Bowser to make Bowser recoil.

"São Paulo's the place, Stuffy," Wilde was enthusing. "It's going to be the Chicago of Brazil. There's big money there, and a sweet life, and I'm going to get my share of it! No rat-race mind you. No bootlicking! Just *easy* . . . just go in and take what you want!"

"Get rich quick, hmm, Bud?"

"What's wrong with it? And even if I don't get rich, there'll be some excitement! Hell, Stuffy, you ought to get yourself a little of that commodity before it's too late. Live!"

For just the most infinitesimal amount of time, with the movement of time in reality suspended for that inch of unreality, Robert had a quite clear picture of his fist connecting with Bud Wilde's jaw—for no reason, just one of those fleeting mental pictures that come as quickly as they go. Then there was silence between them. Their eyes met across the table. Robert knew they were both thinking of the same thing—of the meeting in the corridor earlier that day. Wilde seemed momentarily embarrassed. He played with his swizzle stick and mumbled something about Robert not being able to help what had happened—about being stupid to have wanted to surprise Robert that way. And it was then that Robert should have let go, blurted out so many things: his plans, his past successes at Brown and Forbes, his chance at Something Big, and his caution (even with debts mounting now, and large ones) in waiting for the right moment.

Instead, Robert heard himself making an elaborate defense of the protocol at King & Clary, of the necessity for it, and of the genius of a Wilfred Clary. He raved on and on about his fascination with the intricate workings of King & Clary, of the challenge and excitement, and of the satisfaction he received in his work. There was no clue in his tone, nor in his bearing, that his house in New Hope was at that moment mortgaged for every cent—that nightly he was visited by the tyrannical incubus of his debts—and that now, at last, Robert Bowser was moving in for the Real Kill that would end it all, and was the reason for all of it. The coup was in his sights. He should have told him that.

"So you see," he had concluded, "São Paulo has nothing to offer me."

Just before the turn-off to Lambertville, New Jersey, Robert pulled in at a gas station. Margaret really was asleep now. She was slouched over to the side of the Lincoln, away from Robert, leaning against the window. Her mouth had dropped open slightly, a wisp of her blond hair was bothering her left eye; one hand clutched the Jay Thorpe necklace. Robert stared at her. Part of it, anyway, had been for Margaret, hadn't it? Was it possible that the game had been in control of Robert Bowser, and not Robert in control of the game at all—that Margaret had never been in the least a part of the gambles?

Robert got out and went to the Men's, to splash cold water on his face, to swallow an aspirin for his headache . . . São Paulo . . . He smiled. He imagined the look of utter shock in Bud Wilde's eyes . . . the incredulity in his voice: "$100,000, Stuffy!"

FOUR

"WHEN YOU get to Lambertville," Lois Cutler said, "you just cross over the bridge to New Hope. Turn left and you'll come to the Logan Inn. I'll meet you there."

"In about an hour and a half?"

"Yes, about . . . Can you hear that, Harvey?"

"What?"

"It's Daddy singing 'Boola-Boola!' "

"I don't hear it."

"I'll hold the phone out . . . Did you hear him?"

"Sort of," said Harvey. "The Logan Inn in about an hour and a half."

"Yes . . . Where are you staying, Harvey? With your friends in Princeton?"

"Uh . . . Yes, with my friends."

"I'm glad you're visiting so near. It'll be good to—honestly, now, *my father!* Can you hear him, Harvey?"

"Sort of."

"Oh, God, he's off-key," she giggled. "What a scream!"

"The Logan Inn in about an hour," said Harvey. "I'll be seeing you, Lois."

"Toodle-loo!"

"Toodle . . . Bye!"

It was exactly six when Harvey came out of the phone booth. He looked around for Lake Budde, then walked to the terrace and sat at a table. From his pocket he took his silver cigarette case and a pack of matches from the English Grill in Wilmington, Delaware. The last time he had sent to the P.O. box in New Orleans for matches, he had received three from the English Grill, and two from the Brown Derby in Hollywood. The advertisement had promised that all thirty matchbooks would be different. Harvey had written a severe letter of protest, circling certain words in the advertisement to emphasize their slipshod treatment of him. As yet, there had been no acknowledgment of his letter.

He placed the matchbook from the English Grill face-up, on top his silver cigarette case. When the waiter approached

42

the table, Harvey ordered an Old Smuggler and soda. He had recently taken J&B off his List of Things. It was the KP's favorite brand of Scotch, which was how it had come to be on Harvey's list, but now he wanted a brand that was his. He had looked through copies of *Playboy, Esquire,* and *The New Yorker,* until he had settled on Old Smuggler. He liked the sound of it; in the advertisements for the whisky there was a man in evening clothes, sitting in front of a table of blue glasses numbered 1, 2, 3. Harvey was pleased with the notion he had made "the blue-glass test," that judiciously he had picked a particular Scotch.

From the side pocket of his white jacket, Harvey took out Lois Cutler's most recent letter, and re-read it.

Dear Harvey,
Of course I would like to see you if you are coming East! Mais oui! I feel as though I know you much better than I actually do, and entre ous, Daddy is just a little bit curious about one Monsieur Plangman— the big jealous! He says Plangman is a German name, and he calls you that "Boche"! Is that "redic," or is that ridiculous! R-I-D-I-C-U-L-O-U-S! And I told him so!
Since you ask, Mama is dead. Chez nous we don't discuss the subject. She died when I was two. Poor dumkins took it very hard. My uncle Avery told me Daddy made her have a female doctor all her life, and he even found a female mortician to take her body, since he wanted no other man to ever look at her. Uncle Avery is vice-president of Stowe Chemical, for the record, and à propos de rien.
The best news is that Daddy says I don't have to go to Smith! And—guess what! Daddy says I am due for a little European tour, avec old love-head himself! It is both divine and da-voon, and also glorious, don't you think? We plan the trip for sometime in the fall. Are you green with envy? You never told me whether you've been abroad or not, though I presume you have. Guess who just strolled in! A great big old grizzly bear who wants to know if I'm in the mood for dinner at Chez Odette. (I am!) À propos de bottes, I do not even *know* Tub Oakley that well, much less write him, and I would not believe anything he said about you anyway. You are the first Kappa Pi I've ever gotten to

know, since I dated in the SAE house most of the time I was at Stephens. I don't like Lake Budde either. Do you have a scarlet past that you are so worried? The grizzly bear is trying to read over my shoulder, so I must close and give him a long lecture on grizzly bear behavior. Be sure and look me up if you're passing my way.

Love, Lois.

"Hello there, Plangman," a voice behind Harvey called out. Harvey stood up and put his hand out to Lake Budde.

"What are we—off to the races?" said Budde. He reached across and turned down the collar of Harvey's white jacket.

"What do you mean by that?"

"Sit down, sit down. Don't stand up for me," Budde said. sitting down. "Isn't that Tucker Wolfe's MG out front?"

"Yes. He broke his arm."

"And you drove it East for him, hmm?"

"He asked me to. I'm doing it as a favor to him."

"All right! All right! Did I say anything?"

"It isn't that you said anything, exactly; it's an attitude you have."

"Sit down, Plangman. Don't get so excited. How's Mom P.?"

Harvey sat down. "She's fine."

"What are you drinking?"

"Old Smuggler and soda."

"Umm hmm. I'll have Scotch and soda too."

"What's so funny, Lake?"

"Funny? Nothing. How long did the drive take you?"

"Three days . . . Old Smuggler is a very fine whisky. It took me a long time to decide on it finally."

Lake signaled the waiter and ordered a Scotch and soda. He said, "Wasn't Wilmington a little out of your way?"

"Wilmington where?"

Lake threw his head back and laughed. He said, "The Wilmington where the English Grill is, old man. Jolly fine place, I'm told. Good show and all that, what?"

Harvey picked up the matchbook and put it in his pocket.

"Why, Plangman, old man, you're blushing, by Jove!"

"I'm glad I amuse you, Lake. I always did amuse you, didn't I?"

"You're just such a goddam incorrigible phony, Plangman.

The English Grill of Wilmington, Delaware! Where'd you get it?"

"I was there, for your information. Do you want me to describe it to you, Lake? I can describe it to you."

"Never mind, old chap."

"I don't know why you think I couldn't have been there."

"All things are possible, Plangman."

"Except taking me seriously."

"Except taking you seriously," said Lake, laughing again.

"Another thing," Harvey said, "à propos de rien, just what . . ." but Lake Budde's laughter grew louder, and now he was holding his stomach with one hand, and the table's side with the other, rocking back and forth as he laughed. "A prop-puss dee ry-en," he giggled between bursts of laughter. "A prop-puss de ry-en! I never knew you spoke French, Plangman. I don't think most French people would realize it. *A prop-puss!*"

The waiter served Budde his Scotch then. Budde held his glass up in the gesture of a toast. "Long may you waver, Plangman," he said.

Lake Budde had been last year's Kappa Pi president. Besides Case Bolton, Harvey had envied and admired Budde even more than the others. Budde had a well-bred, wholesome appearance characteristic of certain rich boys—a look that was more Harvard yard than Jesse steps at Missouri—a face that was boyishly handsome, tanned and shiny, with brown hair worn in a sort of wind-blown Prince Charlie style, and bright blue eyes. His grades from boarding school had not been good enough for an Ivy League college; like a lot of Easterners who attended Missouri University because of disqualifying grades, Lake used the excuse that he was interested in journalism. The University of Missouri had one of the best journalism schools in the country. At Missouri, Lake drove a British Sprite convertible, the color of his eyes. He played piano and dated a raven-haired Pi Phi who had been last year's Homecoming Queen, and whenever Harvey had been invited to any of the Kappa Pi functions, it was always Lake who extended the invitation. When Boy Ames' father was killed in an air crash last February, it was Lake who put an arm around his shoulder, led him into the sanctuary of the President's Suite at Kappa Pi, and broke the news to Boy. The other Kappa Pi's had stood around wondering how to approach Boy, but Lake knew how—just as Case Bolton would have known how. Harvey used to watch Lake; it seemed to Harvey that Lake had lived one hundred years longer than most Kappa Pi's, all of whom had seemed to live a good ninety years longer than Harvey. Harvey wondered if sometime during Lake's youth his father, or his mother or someone, had simply instructed him in such a way that nothing could come up he could not handle. He imagined some distinguished-looking gentleman seated in a grand living room of a fine manor house saying calmly to Lake, "Now in the case of a boy losing his father in a disaster, Lake—one simply puts his arm around his shoulder and ..." How else did boys like Lake know so much, if someone had not told them?

After a swallow of his drink, Lake Budde said, "Well, what was the other thing, Harvey?"

"What did you mean when you asked if I was off to the races?"

"Why should I pick on you, ah? Forget it."

"Why *do* you pick on me? It seems to give you pleasure?"

"You ask for it sometimes, Plangman. How's Tub doing with geology?"

"I don't know. Tub Oakley's not my favorite person."

"Who is, Plangman?"

"Who?" Harvey shrugged. "No one you know ... Oh, you probably know them, or know of them. I'm invited there for the weekend."

"Who are they?"

"The Cutlers. The Hayden Cutlers."

"Nope, I don't."

"Your family probably does. They're from New Hope, Pennsylvania."

"Why would my family know them?"

"Well, they're well-off and all. Her maternal grandparents were Bea and William Kemper. Her uncle's a Boocock. We all call him "Boo.""

"Go on."

"What do you mean 'go on'? That's all. Her maternal grandparents were descended from John Alden and Henry Adams."

"Oh! That's fantastic!"

"Well, it is!"

"I'm agreeing with you, Plangman. What else?"

"I don't know why we can't have a simple conversation, Lake. I looked you up as a favor to my mother. Now why can't we just have a simple conversation?"

"Isn't that what we're having?"

"You have this funny attitude."

"I'm sorry, Plangman. I don't happen to know the Cutlers, that's all. How long are you visiting them?"

"I may marry Lois."

"Congratulations."

"You see what I mean?"

"I said, congratulations. What was I supposed to say?"

"She went to Stephens College. Do you know how I met her? Your fraternity brother—Tub Oakley—got so drunk one night, he couldn't take her home. I had to do it."

"That was a lucky break for you."

"I don't need a lucky break to meet people. Is that what you think?"

"I think you've got a chip on your shoulder, Plangman. I think I'll swallow this and be on my way."

"It's just as well," said Harvey. "I'm due there almost immediately."

"Here's to the groom!"

"It's not all settled, by any means."

"Here's luck anyway, Plangman. I'll buy you this drink. Tell Mom hello for me."

"Thank you."

They stood up. Harvey Plangman said, "Lois is a debutante, you know. I'm not much for this society business, but one gets carried along with it."

Lake Budde was placing two dollar bills on top the check. "Umm hmmm. I suppose so."

Lake wore a smart gray-and-white checked poplin jacket, with dark brown linen trousers. As they walked from the terrace through the Inn, Harvey said, "By the by, that's a handsome coat you've got there, Budde."

"Thanks, old boy. Glad you like it."

"As you can see, I'm carrying the white jacket fad East."

"The what?"

"You know," Harvey laughed and touched the lapels of his jacket. "The white jacket fad."

"I noticed."

"Why do you say it that way?"

"Oh, Plangman, forget it."

"I never copied the Kappa Pi's, but I noticed most of them have jackets just like this."

"Umm hmm. I'm parked next to Tucker's car."

"Did you mean my jacket when you said I was off to the races?"

"Will you let anything drop, Plangman?"

Harvey noticed the girl at the desk smiled and nodded to Lake.

Harvey called out, "I'll get that magazine in the city."

The girl nodded, but the smile she gave Harvey was less enthusiastic, more one of curiosity.

"What magazine?" said Lake.

"Fortune," Harvey said. "Earlier while I was waiting for you, she happened to remark that she was sorry they didn't carry *Fortune* or something I might glance at while I was waiting."

"Oh Jesus!" said Budde under his breath.

"She did! I don't know what put it into her head, but. . ."

"She was probably impressed by that goddam white waiter's jacket you've got on, Plangman. She probably figured you were some giant of industry!"

They were at the entranceway now, walking toward the parking lot. Harvey could see the light blue Sprite beside Tucker Wolfe's MG. Harvey said, "Then the jacket's wrong, is that it?"

"Not wrong, just silly."

"But I've seen the Kappa Pi's wear . . ."

"On campus. On *campus,* Plangman!"

"I see."

Lake Budde sighed. "It isn't the end of the world, for Christ's sake. Why don't you just chuck the jacket? And while you're at it, Plangman, chuck that thing sticking in your tie."

"The tie pin?"

"Is that what it is?"

"Maybe I ought to just commit suicide?"

"Harvey," Lake said, standing in front of his Sprite, "I'm not picking on you or anything. Since you asked, I'd chuck the tie pin and the jacket. Jesus, I don't know why you always get me into this sort of situation. You always do. It's like the time you bought the bottle of creme de menthe for our Hink Drink-and-Cook-Out party. I wasn't going to say anything that night either."

"But you did. I remember it very clearly, Lake. You said it wasn't your idea of booze to bring along on a bottle party. You were right, I know that. But it was the way you said it. I've been telling you all along it is this attitude of yours. It's your superior attitude."

"Do you remember vourself at that party, Plangman? You

were going around telling everyone you'd brought the most expensive bottle there! Do you remember that?"

"Still and all . . . still and all."

"Yes, Plangman . . . still and all . . . well, it's been real fine!"

"How do I get to Lambertville from here?" said Harvey.

"Go all the way down to the end of this street. You'll see a sign pointing that way."

"Goodbye then, Lake."

"Ta, ta, old chap!"

"Thanks for the drink," said Harvey, "and thanks for the decent way you informed me that everything I'm wearing is all wrong."

"Don't mention it," Lake Budde said sourly. He started his Sprite with a roar, backed out, extended Harvey a quick, bored salute, and drove off.

FIVE

AT THE gas station in Lambertville, Robert Bowser heard the door of the Men's open and close; then open and close again.

"I'm through here!" he called out, but whoever it was had gone on.

Robert dried his face and hands on the paper towels, shoved them in the disposal can, and then took his glasses from the utility shelf and put them on. As he turned to retrieve his jacket from the chair, he glanced down at a wallet lying on the floor.

It was a light blue wallet made of some sort of plastic material; a new wallet, still shiny and stiff. Robert flipped it open and read the identification card. It belonged to a Harvey Plangman, from 702 Wentwroth Avenue. Columbia, Missouri. After "In Case of Accident Please Notify" was "Sophie Plangman, Kappa Pi House, Columbia, Missouri." The card had been made out in an ornate handwriting with circle-i dots, flourishes, and elaborate capitals, all in purple ink. There was a Missouri driver's license behind one of the celluloid shields, and next to it, a Woolworth employee's identification card. The next shield contained a photograph of a woman in a full skirt and peasant blouse, leaning on an arrow-shaped sign which said Toluca de Lerdo. Across the photograph was written: "Yo te amo! -Gert". Under a third shield was a piece of paper with a list of things scribbled in the same purple ink:

Jaguar XK -140 Sports Roadster
Old Smuggler Scotch
Fortune Magazine
Trumper's Coronis Hair Preparation
Olive green moccasins by Battaglia
Dry Fly Sherry
Gubelin turning globe World-Time clock.
Glove-tanned natural cowhide Kent travel scuffs.
Steerhide, hand-painted game bird den accessories.

Beneath that list was a penciled list headed Vocabulary.

à propos de rien (appropos of nothing)
à propos de bottes (phrase used to change subject)
jejune (dull, insipid)
gerent (one who rules)
sursum corda (Latin toast: lift up your hearts)

In the money compartment was a letter, four or five ten-dollar bills, and a book of matches from Commander's Palace in New Orleans. Robert took all of this in very quickly, not bothering to examine the side pockets. He placed the wallet on the utility shelf above the sink, wondering vaguely if he should wrap the wallet and mail it to the address, or simply leave it with the gas station attendant. It had obviously been dropped by whoever had come into the Men's while Robert was washing up. It was a strange wallet, its contents puzzling. In the mirror above the sink, Robert saw his own reflection momentarily. He had a distinctly owlish look; a very distinct one. He studied himself for a second or so, his lips wide and firm and straight, his brown eyes serious behind the whirls of thick glass—firm jaw, a slightly large, masculine nose, and large ears, close to his head—a thick crop of wavy black hair, with the slight silver-gray tinseling —and now he was frowning. His features would be readily identifiable; the glasses clinched it. Why had he not thought to buy new frames? That would have been little enough help, but with the same old frames anyone who saw his photograph in a newspaper would know he was Robert Bowser. He had done so very little in the way of planning, little more, really, than to arrange for the flight to Brazil, and for the $25,000 in cash. He stared at himself in the mirror, his lips tipping in a bewildered, halfhearted grin of disbelief. No, he could not back down now; on Tuesday the Baker account would show a shortage of three thousand shares, plus the exaggeration of the original King & Clary investment. He was all the way into it now, and he was so unprepared! What crazy bravado had ever sustained him? A silly, sick-sounding chuckle escaped his throat, accompanied by a sudden chill, and a futile and terribly intense wish that he were anyone in the world, anyone but Robert Bowser—that he were, say, Plangman, an employee of Woolworth's. He picked up the wallet and held it in his hand, as though by doing it he would gain something. But he gained nothing and as he turned around to pick up his coat off the men's room chair, he realized he had lost something. He had lost his coat. It was gone, was all. In its place was a white cotton jacket, thrown across the chair so that the blue wallet must have fallen from its pocket. Someone had taken his coat, and with it, his letter to Margaret.

SIX

"AREN'T YOU glad to see me, Harvey?"

"Of course I am!"

"Then why don't you relax? Who do you have to call anyway?"

"Just someone. I'm relaxed, honestly."

"Weren't they home?"

"No, they weren't home," said Harvey. He set his elbows up on the table. The sleeves of the suit coat were almost to his knuckles, so that whether he stood or sat, he had to keep his arms slightly higher than his waist.

"Don't you like it here?" Lois Cutler said. "We could go to the Canal House or Odettes, but the Logan is a more 'fun' place. The local people drink here. Besides, it reminds me of some of the barrooms in Columbia, n'est pas?"

"Oui."

"It's sort of musky, that's it! Musky! It has a sort of musky old beery smell that is both divine and da-voon! Nelson Case was in here the other night. Do you know Nelson Case, the announcer?"

"Yes, I guess I've seen him on television."

"Yes, he's on television a lot. He lives here in New Hope. A lot of celebrities do. Is your call a local call?"

"Sort of local," said Harvey. He had memorized the number. Ax-tel 4-3251. He was good at memorizing things. He memorized this number by thinking of a man named Axtel who was forty-three and had just inherited two-hundred-and-fifty-one thousand dollars.

"Sort of local!" Lois Cutler giggled. "How can a call be sort of local! Maybe I even know the people. Who are they? I bet Daddy knows them if I don't!"

Harvey said, "Oh, they're just some friends I met a while ago in Toluca de Lerdo, Mexico." He raised his glass of Old Smuggler to change the subject. "Sursum corda!" he said.

"Sursum corda!" she said, "My, you are mysterious. A propos de rien, Monsieur Plangman, daddy says he never

53

heard of a Colonel Plangman, not in World War II, anyway.
Daddy was in Washington then. He knew a lot of military
personnel and . . ."

"You want to know something amusing, Lois?" Harvey interrupted. "I just had drinks with a frat brother. Lake
Budde. Well, we were sitting around on the terrace of the
Princeton Inn, and Lake was asking my opinion on a good
sherry. I prefer Dry Fly, but that's beside the point. The
point is—suddenly he said what you just said, only you know
how he pronounced it? He pronounced it a prop-puss de
ry-en!"

"A prop-puss de ry-en! Oh, how ridic! Weren't you embarrassed?"

"I was too embarrassed to correct him," said Harvey.

Lois repeated the phrase and laughed and laughed, and
Harvey looked at the clock. He thought: *A man named Ax-
tel who was forty-three inherited two hundred and fifty-one
thousand dollars.* He did not like leaving his name with the
woman who answered the phone; he simply said he would
call back, and then hung up. Already he had tried Robert
Bowser's number three times. The address was River Road,
Lumberville, Pennsylvania. Lois had explained that Lumberville was like a suburb of New Hope. It was a piece of luck
that he was that close to Bowser's home. It made up for the
clumsy mishandling of his impulse to pick Bowser's jacket off
the chair in the Men's at Lambertville. He had not gone in
there with anything in mind but to discard the waiter's
jacket. When he had seen the man in shirtsleeves, bent over
the wash bowl, his suit coat across the chair, he had acted
fast. It was a beige-colored linen suit coat, single button.
Frantically, Harvey had grabbed it, dropping his own jacket
in its place, moving as quickly as he could, out the door and
across to the MG. He raced down the hill into Lambertville, his heart banging under his shirt, his mind whirling.
When he collected his wits, on the 15 m.p.h. ride across
the bridge to New Hope, he realized his wallet was still in
his jacket. Until he found sanctuary in another Men's, at
the Logan Inn, he did not know what the contents were of
the jacket he had stolen.

". . . are you going to be around?" Lois Cutler was saying.

"I'm sorry. What did you say?"

"You seem so nervous, Harvey. I said, how long are you
going to be around?"

"I'm not too sure. I'd certainly like to meet your father."

"Poor dumkins is in New York today. Maybe you can come to dinner tomorrow. Do you mind driving back and forth from Princeton?"

"I may stay here tonight."

"Here?"

"Not here. In New Hope."

"I'd ask you to stay at our place, but with Daddy gone. . . ."

"No, no, no," said Harvey. "I didn't mean anything like that."

"I didn't think you did, but . . ."

"No, of course not! Not in the absence of the gerent, after all."

"You know, Harvey, I honestly think you have one of the best vocabularies of any man I've ever met. Are all the Kappa Pi's like you?"

"Very few Kappa Pi's are like me," said Harvey. "Lois, look, would you mind if I tried that number again?"

"Pas de tout, cheri."

"I'll be right back," said Harvey rising, making sure to keep his arms above his waist.

The same woman answered the phone.

"I'm not the maid, you know," she said. "This is the fourth time you've called, without leaving your name. For your information, sir, this is Mother Franklin. Anything you have to . . ."

Harvey let the arm of the phone drop back in its cradle. From the inside pocket of the linen jacket, he removed the envelope-sized billfold. From the money compartment, he took out the letter. Then he reread it.

My dear Margaret,

By the time you receive this, I will be out of the country.

Shortly after you receive this, the police will be around with questions. You won't have any answers to those questions. The facts will simply have to speak for themselves.

I have embezzled exactly $100,043.77 from King & Clary in the last five years.

After your initial shock, I believe you will probably find it not too hard to believe, after all. Our marriage began on this note, and now it ends on it.

I will supply you with the answer to one question you will undoubtedly be asked. What did he spend the money on?

The answer to that is around you, on you, and above you. (I trust you are reading this letter in the solarium, where you always open your mail, directly under Mother Franklin's room).

You, Margaret, are certainly not to blame for any of it. I exaggerated my income—the directorships, all of it, as you'll undoubtedly soon learn.

Several times (the two instances you know of—this, and the first, are not the only ones) I was quite successful. As Dryden very accurately put it:

> *"Ill habits gather by unseen degrees,*
> *As brooks made rivers, rivers run to seas."*

Now there is a sea around us, and very little else I can say to make things either worse or better.

Robert.

Along with the letter in the money compartment of the billfold, was twenty-two dollars. There was no photograph in the billfold; there were six credit cards, a Pennsylvania driver's license, and a registration card for a new Lincoln Continental. On a slip of paper was the address of a man in São Paulo, Brazil, and a notation of a flight number on Varig Airlines, leaving Idlewild at seven-thirty on this coming Sunday night. There was also a bank book, showing a withdrawal of $25,000, across the face of which was stamped Account Closed.

It was now Friday—nine-thirty, by the clock outside the phone booth.

SEVEN

CHEZ ODETTE was on the River Road, just outside New Hope. As they approached it, Margaret was saying, ". . . because now I'm out of the mood to fix something from the freezer. And there isn't a single thing you can do about your coat or your wallet! We'd just go home, and you'd brood."

"I can't eat dinner in my shirtsleeves, and I can't wear this idiotic jacket!"

"I've seen men in Odette's in short-sleeved sports shirts, Robert. It's summer and this is a resort town. Besides, I'll tell Odette myself that someone picked up your jacket by mistake."

"I don't see how it could have been by mistake. There was no one in there when I went in, and the door just opened and closed. When I turned around . . ."

Margaret sighed. "You weren't carrying more than twenty dollars, and that coat is three years old. It's not as bad as you're making it seem."

"Oh, no! It isn't that bad at all."

"Well, it isn't! Robert, I feel like having a good dinner. It'll do you good, too."

"All right," Robert said. "We'll have to charge it.

"So we have to charge it!" Margaret answered; she shrugged her shoulders as though the whole matter was an irritating bore.

Robert let her off at the entranceway, and drove around to the side to park. Margaret was right; there was nothing he could do about it. The worst part was that he could not remember whether or not he had sealed and stamped the letter to Margaret. If he had, there was a slim chance that he was safe——that whoever had picked up his coat (stolen it? what?) would simply deposit the letter in a mailbox, as Robert would do if he were in the same situation. Nothing about the incident tallied. If it were Plangman who had taken his coat, why would he have left his behind,

with his wallet still in it? The only answer Robert could
come up with was that perhaps the fellow was drunk;
perhaps he had not known what he was doing. The attendant at the gas station could not remember seeing another car pull in. There were simply no clues, not a one.
Either Robert Bowser was ruined, right now at this very
moment, or things were still at the same head.

His headache was much worse now; accompanying it was
a feeling of castastrophic indifference, as though a numb-
ness had set in, and while he could appreciate the im-
minent danger, he could not feel it, nor bring himself to
assess its outcome.

Odette greeted him with a big smile, "Darling, I'm zo
zorry about ze coat, but na-vair mind now!"

He smiled back, then spotted Margaret at a table in front
by the bar. Edith and Arthur Summers were finishing dinner
a few tables away, and the moment Robert joined Margaret she said, "I've asked the Summers over for a drink,
dear. Buy them a Remy Martin or something. Edith
wouldn't let me pay for my lunch when we ate at the
Logan last week."

Robert nodded, sighed.

"Well, I had to, Robert," said Margaret.

"It's all right."

"They'll cheer us up."

Arthur and Edith Summers were always depressingly
cheerful, filled with small talk which they engaged in with
zestful enthusiasm, as though there were nothing in the
world as fascinating as the fact that it might rain tomorrow.
Arthur Summers owned Arpedia Swimming Pools, in
Quakerstown, Pennsylvania, and Edith was one of the many
Bucks County matrons who fell into the category of being
"interested in the arts." This could mean almost anything:
that she had taken the adult class in ceramics at the high
school last fall, that she had purchased an abstract Ent-
whistle from Charles IV gallery three weeks ago, or that
she was a committee chairman for the Book Review Hour
of The New Hope Ladies' Lawn Improvement Guild. Arthur and Edith were both tall and thin and graying; both
wore rimless glasses and looked more like brother and sister
than man and wife. At cocktail parties, Edith could be re-
lied on to explain that she never drank gin martinis because
gin made her break out, and Arthur was predictably solicitous toward her after her third drink of anything, his admon-

ishments invariably beginning, "Now, now, Mommy, we'd better go easy."

"Robert wants to buy you a brandy," said Margaret as they sat down. "We've just come in from New York."

"Mommy's had enough, I think. I'll have a quickie. Then we have to run along."

"Daddy's going to New York tomorrow," said Edith Summers, "and I have to drive to Chalfont for the Sautersly auction."

Was it all as simple as it sounded? Were there undertows in the Summers' life? The waitress appeared and Robert ordered two martinis and a brandy. What if he were simply to give in all the way now? To say simply, "I suppose I ought to tell you something, Arthur and Edith, and you too, Margaret." He imagined himself giving in to this impulse, wondered if just that much control kept him from ruin, or if already the wheels of his ruin were in motion— if the letter he had written Margaret was right now spread out on someone's table. He played with the idea of Arthur Summers having a similar letter somewhere, or Arthur thinking about it as they were all sitting there chatting. He looked carefully at Summers. Summers' eyes met his for a brief instant. Brothers or not, Robert thought?"

"I had lunch at the Drake this noon," Margaret was saying, "and everyone in New York calls very dry martinis *white* martinis. They charge 10¢ extra for them."

"Of course they'd have to," Arthur Summers chuckled. "They're probably all gin."

Edith Summers smiled like a child receiving a colored gum drop. "White martinis! I've never heard them called that before."

"You better forget you ever heard it," Arthur chuckled again.

"Oh, Daddy's right. I get the hives from gin. My doctor says I'm allergic to gin, and that's all there is to it! Now, it's very peculiar, because I can drink vodka. I've had vodka screwdrivers, vodka martinis, vodka and tonic—anything with vodka. I can handle vodka, but not gin. Gin gives me hives the size of half dollars, all over my body."

"That's perfectly true," said Arthur Summers.

"I just can't drink it."

"How are things at King & Clary, Robert?" Arthur asked.

So it went—so it went. Robert heard himself answering questions, asking them—exclaiming, remarking—all the while his thoughts teased him with suggestive impulses, dallied around the fringes of the crisis, and cried for control. The waitress arrived with the drinks, and Robert noticed that the piano player was sitting down now; he pitied himself immensely, imagining how the music would compound the pain in his head. In the rear pocket of his trousers he was aware of the bulge of Harvey Plangman's wallet.

Margaret said, "Edith, are you positive you won't have a brandy?"

"Oh no, thank you. I have to drive to an auction in Chalfont tomorrow, and Daddy's going into New York."

"*You Said That,*" Robert's head screamed. He smiled at Edith.

"The Sautersly auction," she smiled back.

"Well, cheers!" Margaret held up her martini. "No, wait," she said. "Robert's had such rotten luck on the way out—there's an old Irish toast. You know, Robert, remember it? Why don't we cheer ourselves up; you say that toast, hmm?"

Robert held up his glass. He recited the toast, feigning a tone of mild gaiety. In the mirror behind Margaret he could see his face, he could see it framed in the black lines of newsprint—EMBEZZLER CAUGHT!? . . . EMBEZZLER AT LARGE!? . . . "May the wind always be at your back!" he recited to his reflection, "May you always take the right turn in the road! May God take a liking to you, but not too soon."

Edith Summers was making squeaks of delight, and Arthur murmured, "very good," "very good," while the, glasses clinked and separated. Then Robert heard Margaret saying, "What's the matter, Robert?"

He had been sitting there holding his glass, without drinking from it. He had been stopped in his thoughts, at the point in the toast where he had wished that one always take the right turn in the road. As clearly as when he had seen it earlier that day, Robert saw in his mind's eye the run-down, squat, two-story gray shingle house on Route 22 out of Somerville. Just for an instant he saw it, and in that microscopic space of time, he saw himself turning the broken mailbox right side up, straightening it on its post.

"A penny for them?" said Edith Summers.

Robert forced a smile. "I was just dreaming," he said.

He sipped the martini; the piano player began a very saccharine rendition of "Look To The Rainbow," and a pe-

tite red headed girl standing at the piano sang along with
the music.

After the Summers left, Robert ordered escargots for
Margaret and himself, and a bottle of cold Mersault. Margaret was very quiet, a sign she was carefully selecting the
right words for a serious discussion with Robert. She was
quiet and she was playing with her wedding ring, all the
signs Robert needed to warn him that Margaret was thinking about them. Robert's headache was nearly anesthetized
by the gin now, but he was not up to one of their dis-
cussions, and he tried to head it off. He started a conversation about the dinner party Margaret had planned for next
week, pleased with his ability to carry it off so well. He
found himself talking with ease about the food and other
practical details. Maybe it would all work out. The letter
to Margaret went from the table on which it had been
spread out, back into the envelope; now, still sealed, it was
being slipped down the slit of a mailbox. Tomorrow morning, just in case, Robert would go down to the box for their
mail.

Normally Margaret could talk and talk about the arrangements for a party; about the seating arrangements,
about the provisions for shelter in case of rain, if they
were having a largeish (Margaret's word) crowd, about
whether or not to hire Kenneth to serve drinks (he was
quick and polite, but took home bags of food at the end)
or Mrs. Johnston (who took nothing home but the great
quantity of liquor she sneaked throughout an evening, each
drink making her a bit nastier). Margaret, Robert soon
learned, was disinterested even in the party now. She had
something to say to Robert, and she began the moment the
waitress poured the Mersault.

"Robert, is it that you think Clary is testing you with this
Baker assignment?"

"No, it was always in the offing."

"You're just acting so strangely. I've been thinking about
that remark you made ever since we left Somerville. It's
almost as though you were looking for some sort of security."

"Margaret, I said I loved you because I just happened
to feel like it. What's wrong with telling your wife you love
her?"

"I agree, it's certainly in order. But what made you think
of it at that particular moment?"

"I don't even remember now. I don't even remember what we were discussing."

"I was just saying that I thought we'd go back to round butter balls."

"Maybe I wasn't listening carefully. I was probably daydreaming."

"Well, Robert, it isn't like you to daydream——and then come up with a remark like that. It isn't like you."

"Oh, Margaret, I don't know."

"I'm not picking on you, dear. I'm worried. Then this business of losing your coat. The anxiety over that coat! I watched your face while we° drove from Lambertville. It isn't like you."

"You know me pretty well, don't you?"

"Of course, dear. That's why I'm so concerned."

"The wine has been over-chilled," said Robert.

His voice seemed to come from a very long way off. Some horrible bore had said those words. He could see the whole thing, see himself sitting at a table saying the wine was over-chilled, while an odd collection of floating figures hovered above, smiling——smirking? Bud Wilde, holding his battered hat with the weather stains on the band——the window washer with his checkered cap and his big button——and then, someone else——an owlish look to his countenance—— the firm jaw and the large ears. He winked at Robert Bowser. "It won't be long now, pal," he promised.

"I know it is," Margaret was saying. "No one ever chills wine anymore. They simply keep it in the icebox. Robert, I'm worried about you."

"I'm sorry. I have a headache tonight."

"Maybe instead of the party, we should go to Nassau when you get back. I'd love to take mother too. We all need a vacation."

"Margaret, just don't worry. There's nothing to worry about. There's nothing at all to worry about." The words came from some cavern in his mind, sweet and sure, plain and perfectly logical. Even Robert was comforted by them. He said, "Things always work out. It's very simple."

Margaret looked immensely relieved. "Yes," she smiled. "I must be a little on edge myself. You know, Robert, I want you to be a vice-president very badly. It's important for you, and high time. I'm afraid I get a little tense myself, I want it so badly for you."

"Of course you do. I'm sorry if I didn't appreciate. . ."

"No, I'm sorry. It's just that it's every bit as important to me as it is to you."

"There now, feel better?" Robert said, pouring some of the Mersault into her glass.

"Much, much better. But you were acting strangely, you know. I know you better than you know yourself, Robert."

"Yes, perhaps you do."

"Of course I do, dear!"

They worked on their escargots for awhile. Robert did not trust himself to look closely at her until some moments had passed, though he wanted to. He almost believed he would see a complete stranger. Earlier, he had felt that, but when he looked, she was as familiar as his own face. He waited a bit, then he did look closely at her. There was the same sense of estrangement that there had been before, and the same feeling as before, that he must be going to miss her, mustn't he? She was what he knew. Yes, he could predict her—when she would light a cigarette and when she wouldn't—the vein that throbbed near her temple when she was tired—the way, after love-making, she always asked him to check to see if the front yard light were out (as though the abandonment of physical intercourse had made them abandoned in other ways, so abandoned the front yard light might burn all night)—her reaction to this person, that news story, his moods—all the predictable things one person learns about another in over twenty-one years. And yet—yet it was all on the surface, the same as her knowledge of him was. If things worked according to plan, Monday morning she would know a great deal more about him than he would ever know about her. He sat there looking at his wife, and wondering: did she too, at some point in an evening, remember something that was inexplicably secret, some part of her experience that she held inside her—a face, a voice, some piece of a day that would come back to her, and momentarily seduce her interest— so that she too would be left with the cocktail glass held in a toast, her mind gone to some other place, her spirit bewildered by the incident; even tantalized or afraid? Could it be even now, that she was sitting opposite Robert wondering the very same thing about him?

"I think I figured it out," Margaret said then.

"Figured what out?"

"Do you remember that we decided to have dinner out

before I got on the subject of round butter balls? Remember?"

"I guess go."

"I think you were pleased, Robert. Do you know that it's been a very long time since we've been alone together? We've always had Mother with us."

"Quite right."

"Now, you won't admiṭ it, but I think Mother irritates you at times. No, I really think so, Robert."

"Well—it's a possibility."

"Of course it is! We should try to be by ourselves occasionally. We'll make a point to," Margaret said gaily. "All right, dear?"

"All right, Margaret."

"That's what was behind that remark!" said Margaret.

EIGHT

"So I said, now listen, I am not the maid, for your information. I said, 'This is Mother Franklin!' "

"Robert," Margaret said, "perhaps it was someone calling about your coat."

"Yes, I was thinking that myself."

"He called five times. I counted. Five times. I said, 'If you would simply leave your name, Mr. Bowser will call you when he gets in.' I said, 'This is Mother Franklin, not the maid.' "

The three of them were standing in the kitchen. Margaret was heating milk for Mother Franklin's Ovaltine, while Robert got down the package of marshmallows. Mother Franklin was wearing one of Margaret's Hawaiian muumuus, instead of her own nightgown, and Margaret's tangerine nylon tricot robe, with the satin buttons and satin piping. She knew Margaret disliked having her wear her clothes. If she were left alone in the house for very long, she took it out on Margaret this way. If Margaret were to buy Mother Franklin a Hawaiian muumuu of her own, or a tangerine robe, Mother Franklin would only insist that the styles were too young for her, and refuse to wear them. Mother Franklin was a short, wiry, white-haired old woman who seemed to shrink a little more every day. When she wore sweaters—and she often did, with skirts and saddle shoes and bobby socks—the sweaters hung as though they were put over a clothes hanger. Yet this wizened old woman's tiny body contained an iron will, and a stubbornness and nerve that made Robert often wish he could simply step down on hard, with his foot, the same way one killed a persistent and pesty bumblebee. He and Margaret had come home to find Mother Franklin in a nervous rage over the telephone calls. The least little thing could set her off; this time, she was positive that the caller did not believe she was trustworthy enough for him to leave a message. The fact was, Mother Franklin often forgot telephone messages. Robert was sure that somewhere in the back of her mind was the fantasy that Robert and Margaret had told their friends never to leave a message with Mother Franklin when they called, since she was not reliable. She ranted on about the kind of people who telephone without giving their name, and whined to Margaret that she needed some hot chocolate to help her sleep. Her white hair was rolled around large wire curlers, and she was barefoot; her toenails were painted with Margaret's red nail polish.

"Did he say he'd call back?" Robert asked her.

"He did not!"

"Well, I hope you told him we'd be in soon?"

"I told him nothing! I said, 'This is Mother Franklin and not the maid.' "

"It must have been about the coat," said Margaret. "Here, Robert," handing him the Ovaltine, "would you put a marshmallow in that for Mother?"

Robert took the cup and dropped the marshmallow in it. "And he didn't say anything else, hmm, Mother Franklin? He just asked for me?"

Mother Franklin shrieked, "Don't stir it! I don't like my marshmallow stirred in! I like it to float on top!"

"Mother, don't shout, please!" Margaret said.

"Why did he have to stir it?" Mother Franklin complained. "He knows I like it floating on top! Now, it's all mixed in the way I hate it!"

Robert left the cup on the kitchen table and walked out of the room. Behind him he heard Margaret shushing his mother-in-law, heard her purring about Robert's Winston-Salem assignment, about the likelihood of Robert's vice-presidency. "We'll all go to Nassau for a vacation, to celebrate!" he heard Margaret say, and Mother Franklin said, "The hospital's where I'm going! My cramps are back again, and the pains down my legs, Margaret."

In the front room (Margaret always called it the solarium) Robert walked across to his desk. He took Plangman's wallet from his back pocket and placed it in the top drawer. He paused then, looking down at the wallet. He had not searched it thoroughly; there was a letter in the money compartment which he had not examined, and he had not gone into the wallet's side pockets. Robert leaned across his desk and snapped on his drafting lamp. He sank into the softness of his green-cushioned desk chair and placed the wallet in front of him. From the hallway he could hear the sounds of Margaret and Mother Franklin going upstairs to bed.

The right side pocket of the wallet contained air mail stamps and a Trojan, a matchbook (empty) from the Brown Derby in California, and a page torn from a magazine of some sort, with four verses to a song called "Kappa Pi Pinning Serenade." From the left side pocket of the wallet, Robert removed a folded piece of stationery headed COLUMBIA BUSINESS-SECRETARIAL SCHOOL, COLUMBIA, MISSOURI.

"My darling, dearest, adorable, big, beautiful———" and then an obscenity. Robert stopped at the obscenity. He put the piece of paper aside. He did not refold it and put it back in the left side compartment, but brushed it to the edge of his desk blotter. An uncomfortable feeling came over him —a feeling that this Plangman fellow would not be a very pleasant person to know. He flipped the shields to the driver's license; the Missouri license contained no birthdate, no identifying physical characteristics. Then from the money compartment, he took out the letter. He opened it and read it.

Dear Harvey, Of course I would like to see you if you are coming East. Mais oui!

When he came to the part about the "grizzly bear" who wanted to take the writer to Chez Odette for dinner, his heart jumped. He grabbed the envelope and read the return address. Cutler—Sugan Road—New Hope, Pennsylvania. The name was not familiar. He reached across his desk for the phone book. There was a listing for a Hayden Cutler on Sugan Road. VOlunteer 2-5408.

Uncle Avery is a vice-president of Stowe Chemical.

He sat there, his thoughts ricocheting back and forth. Plangman sounded like a young man. Although there were no fraternities where Robert had gone to college, Kappa Pi was as famous a fraternity as Sigma Chi. Was Plangman a college boy, possibly working his way through college (which would explain the Woolworth employee's card)? If he were a college boy, wouldn't there be a better chance that Robert's letter to Margaret would go unread? Robert felt that was true. He should simply pick up the phone and call the VOlunteer number—explain that he had lost his coat, that there had been a mix-up, that he had Plangman's coat. He knew Stowe Chemical; it was a big and very substantial organization. Robert felt as though his coat and his wallet with the letter were in good hands—restrained hands. He picked up the telephone and dialed the number. He waited through eleven rings, then dropped the arm back in its craddle. For a moment he sat there. The palms of his hands were wet and warm; he could feel the perspiration soak his shirt. Finally, he reached for the other letter—the note— whatever it was. He leaned back and read it.

"My darling, dearest, adorable, big, beautiful—"

The letter was filled with obscenities. In the lewdest language Robert had ever read anywhere, outside of outright pornography, it cajoled, reminisced, promised, begged, and grieved. Clearly, it was not pornography. Gertrude, its writer, had no salacious intent. It was quite simply a love letter, a glorious and foul celebration of the most intimate method of communication between a man and a woman. It was wholly without subterfuge. It was blatant, screaming, weeping, puling, singing. While Robert read it, and while he sat there after he had read it, his entire being was swept with something akin to longing—not a longing for the flesh, or for the touch or sound or sight of anyone he knew; it was more like a homesickness suffered by some orphan who had no particulars with which to fill the framework of the feeling. He thought of the few letters Margaret had written to him, and of his to Margaret. He saw himself in a sudden, distilled, rapid pageant of his years—Robert Bowser—languid and divinable, a cog of ostensible conformity, bloodless and heal- thy as fresh white snow. Only in the Big Gamble was he dif- ferent—and again the thought occurred to him that the game controlled him—even in that way, he was a cog.

Certain ideas of his rang out in his thoughts, the every- day ideas that he had always thought of as his facade—that he now suspected were simply his way of life, and would be, despite the coup. With each idea, there was a scene he could see himself in—standing in a haberdashery now, dis- carding the ties that were too flashy (never give a clue to the bright thread of recklessness, not even in a tie), and now in a restaurant studying the wine list (no, Hermitage Blanc is wrong with squab; better a Bordeaux), now at King & Clary's ("In my investigation, sir, the company's major capital project is a potash mine and plant in Saskatchewan, op- erated by a subsidiary. The plant is ..."), and now in bed with Margaret, embraced by her, the ritual familiar and pre- cise, waiting for the last low moan of ecstasy(?) before it was time for him to deliver himself, the apogee of control, partner in their antiseptic joy.

He could shut his eyes, lean back, and then see his shoes upstairs in the closet, row upon row, shoes for formal, semi-formal, business, spectator sports, all polished and containing their trees; then, open his eyes and see beside his drafting lamp, the red tea cannister made into an over-scale lamp with a grass-color cloth shade, for occasions when more light was necessary. Yes, he had discussed it quite seriously with Margaret; sometimes the drafting lamp was not sufficient, and Margaret had found just the right one for the solarium's decor. Both had sat over drinks in the solarium admiring it. It was the focal point of the whole room, Margaret said.

Above Robert's desk was the Modigliani self-portrait, circa 1918, a little-known drawing Robert had bought for an anniversary gift to the house years ago. He could remember—he could see himself in his memory—sitting with Margaret on the sofa beside him, while he discussed Brancusi's influence on Modigliani; it was a night who knows in what year, when they had first made frozen daiquiris in their new Waring blender.

Robert stuffed the letter from Gertrude back in Plangman's wallet. São Paulo—the words sounded suddenly menacing, as though the leap from here to there was too large, and there was not time enough to fit into his new role. It was too soon to go so far from what he knew, from what had held him, almost in bondage, throughout his life. São Paulo—foreign, a bright thread, which was, after all, only a thread—and not much to go on.

The sharp sound of the ringing telephone punctuated this thought. His hand trembled as he took his chances.

"Mr. Bowser?"

"Yes."

"Mr. Bowser, my name is Harvey Plangman."

"Yes, Mr. Plangman. I have your wallet, and jacket too, I believe."

"I have yours, Mr. Bowser."

"Where are you?"

"I'm at the Black Bass, here in Lumberville."

"Why don't you drive over here? Do you have a car? I could offer you a drink, and we could reclaim our things."

"I have a car, sir. Is your family there?"

"Yes, but it's only ten-thirty. No one's asleep."

"Is this a private line? Do you have an extension?"

"It's quite private."

"Mr. Bowser, were you planning to go to Brazil?"

"What are you talking about?"

"I'm talking about the sea around you, Mr. Bowser."

"I see."

"You don't have anything to be afraid of, Mr. Bowser."

"I'd better come there."

"Yes, I think it would be much better if you came here."

"I'll be there in fifteen minutes."

"You'll know who I am, all right, Mr. Bowser. I'm wearing your coat."

"Fifteen minutes," said Robert.

Upstairs, Margaret was giving Mother Franklin a back rub.

"Don't try to peek in and see me," said Mother Franklin. "I haven't a stitch on!"

"Oh, Moth-ther!" Margaret giggled.

Robert stood in the doorway. "That was the man who has my coat and wallet," he said. "He called from the Black Bass. I'm going to run over there."

"You should have invited him here, Robert."

"If he's not the sort to leave his name when he telephones," Mother Franklin said, "he's not the sort to ask to the house. I told him, 'I'm not the maid here, I'm Mother Franklin.'"

"All right! All right!" Robert snapped. "I'll be back in a little while."

"Robert?"

"Yes, Margaret."

"Was it the same man whose wallet you have?"

"Yes, the same one."

"Well, that's grand, isn't it? It was all a mistake, it's very simple."

"You're rubbing my ribs too hard!" Mother Franklin shouted. "You're taking it out on me because I wore your muumuu, aren't you, Margaret?"

Oh God, Robert prayed, don't let me miss moments like this; don't let what's in store for me now, be bad enough for me to wish I were back here. He went down the stairs, Mother Franklin's voice rasping his ears. "Oh, yes, you are; yes; you are, Margaret, you're mad at me for wearing your muumuu!"

NINE

"AND IF I don't agree to your plan?" Robert Bowser asked.

"Please, Mr. Bowser, I don't want to threaten you."

"That's what blackmail is all about," said Bowser.

He studied Harvey Plangman carefully. He knew his kind, all right; you couldn't miss his kind. When Bowser had first come into the bar, he had noticed Plangman's stare. He was taking in everything right down to the shoes. It was as though suddenly Bowser were wearing price tags on everything, as though the labels on his clothes were all sewed on the outside. There was in his eyes that peculiar mixture of envy and hero-worship, indigenous to Plangman's kind. And then—Plangman's plan—a strange way to blackmail a man. An oddly inviting plan, it was, except that it depended on Bowser's trusting Harvey Plangman. There was the catch.

. Harvey Plangman said, "Mr. Bowser, can't we discuss this in a friendly way? Do you know, I liked you from the start—from the moment you walked in here. You look sort of like that Martin Gabel on 'What's My Line?' "

"I wouldn't know," Bowser sighed. It was like a dream, this whole thing. Not a nightmare either. Simply fantastic, unreal.

"He's Arlene Francis' husband," said Plangman. "Only you're thinner. Mr. Bowser, I know you didn't think much of me when you first saw me. I saw the way you looked at me. Do you remember?"

"No."

"I'm used to it, so it's all right. I get that kind of a look nine times out of ten. That's why this whole thing is so important to me, sir. But the part that makes me happiest, is that I'll be doing you a favor too. You need a place to hide for awhile—a comfortable place where you'll be safe. Sir, 702 Wentwroth is that place, believe me. So I'll be doing you a favor, and in turn, I'll have a chance to get my room at the top. Did you see that movie, sir, 'Room At The Top'?"

71

"No, I didn't."

"I saw it three times. It won the Academy Award. You must not be the type for TV and movies, is that it?"

"Mr. Plangman, will you please stop skirting around the subject?"

"But your likes and dislikes are part of the subject, sir."

"If I don't agree to your plan, you'll go to the police. That's right, isn't it?"

"We can help each other, sir. Don't you see that? My first suggestion is that you go into New York City tomorrow and get yourself some rimless glasses. After you get to Missouri, you can change to contact lenses. Get a brush cut and grow a mustache. You might even try a beard. In Columbia, a man with a beard is not too unusual. Many of the professors have beards. What do you think I should do first? Remember, I want to make a very good impression on Hayden Cutler tomorrow night! Perhaps I should wear something special."

Robert Bowser said, "The $25,000 withdrawn from my savings was sent on to São Paulo, Plangman." It was a lie, of course. The $25,000 was it; it was in cash, back at the house, zipped into Robert Bowser's tie case.

"Don't drag it out longer than you have to, sir," Harvey Plangman said, glancing about the terrace of the Black Bass Inn, at the view of the Delaware Canal, and the lights along the bank. "It's pleasant here, but I'm not sure we want to stay until closing. There's too much to do, don't you agree?"

"You're convinced I have it, aren't you?"

"Do you know I've never had more than $250 in the bank at one time, Mr. Bowser? I felt rich when I had that much! Don't you see how unfair it is? You've gone through 100,000—pffft! Like that! You may even still have it, or more. I can only go by the bank book. I'm only asking for $10,000. A drop in the bucket, sir, don't you agree?"

Yes, Bowser knew his kind. Big risks for small gains. It was ironical that his kind would be the stumbling-block now, that the epitome of all that Bowser had guarded himself against becoming, would present himself at the eleventh hour, stand in his way and grin—and call him "sir."

Bowser said, "Just $10,000, and control over my movements, that's all you're asking."

"$10,000 and your guidance, sir. Put it that way."

"My guidance!"

"Don't laugh at me, Mr. Bowser. It's not very pleasant to be laughed at, you know."

"My guidance, ha!"

"Isn't it clear yet? I want to enter your world, sir. The money isn't enough. Even if I were to ask you for twice the amount, it wouldn't be enough. Nor would $100,000. I need direction, advice—someone to tell me what to wear and say and do. Guidance, Mr. Bowser—a few pointers. Look sir, if I can just have ten thousand dollars and a few pointers, I know I can marry Lois Cutler before the winter."

"Where do you think that will get you, Plangman?"

"Where I want to go—into your world."

"Just like that, eh?" Bowser said, with a snap to his fingers. That was like the Plangmans of this world, all right. Hopelessly like them. What they wanted, they wanted fast, and they were not even sure what they would get. It was the difference between greed and ambition. Bowser sighed again, frustrated by Plangman's ignorance. He said, "For one thing, Plangman, I'm not in some special world, with Hayden Cutler, Rockefeller, Paul Getty and the Vanderbilts. There's no world like that. You're so ill-informed, it's preposterous. I don't know how to talk with you."

"Preposterous? I don't think so. Wait a minute. I have something here." Plangman took a pencil from his pocket, and wrote on the matchbook of the English Grill. "There!" he said, passing it across to Robert Bowser. "Suppose you were to come across these abbreviations. They were listed after Lois' uncle's name in the Register, the Social Register, sir."

"Well, what about them?"

"Un, Ln, B, Pg, H. What do they mean?"

"Union Club, Links Club, Brook Club, and Harvard, I suppose," said Bowser. "I don't know the Pg offhand."

"The Pg. is The Pilgrims, sir. But you got four out of five."

"What are you getting at? Why are you off on all these tangents?"

"Don't be impatient, sir, please! I'm simply proving that you are in the same world as Lois, at any rate. When I saw those abbreviations, I didn't know what a one meant! Not a one, sir!"

"I don't belong to any of those clubs, and I'm not in the Register."

"Neither is Hayden Cutler. Both you and Hayden Cutler know about those things, though. Were you born with those facts in your heads? No, no! But you were born into that world! Well, I wasn't! I need to be tutored, sir!"

"And you think that if you do manage to marry Lois Cutler, her father will share his wealth with you! Well, don't make that mistake, Mr. Plangman. Don't make that mistake!"

"I'm not after money, I'm really not! I'm after class! Over and over I tell myself how unfair it is—that some people are simply born with it—that others, like me, Mr. Bowser, are expected to sit around on the sidelines and shrug our shoulders and tell ourselves that that's just the way the ball bounces—too bad, and all that rot! I'm tired of it, Mr. Bowser! My God, you don't know how sick and tired of it I am! And you, sir, born with it, and it wasn't enough. No, you had to have $100,000 in the deal!"

"I wasn't born with—class."

"Where did you attend college, sir?"

"Princeton."

"Ummm hmm. Princeton. Ivy League."

"All sorts of young men go to Princeton. It means nothing—nothing."

"It means, sir, that their mothers don't run boarding houses, that they don't sleep on the couches of their living rooms, and that they know things. Things! Dammit, I'm not giving you a sob story. I just want to point out that what I want isn't so fantastic! I'm not trying to marry into the Rockefeller family, and maybe my idea of class isn't yours. The rich can always think of somebody richer—that's the great part about being rich, you can be so modest. But if you're poor, Mr. Bowser, or if you're sick, it's very hard to think of someone poorer or sicker. You just don't feel inclined to!"

"You don't want to be rich, you said."

"That's right, Mr. Bowser. Class! That's A-number 1. Class! I guess you think I'm primitive, hmm?"

"I think you're crazy," said Robert Bowser. "No one can give you class. I'd be the last person . . . I know very little about people like the Cutlers. The whole damned thing is . . ."

"Is what, sir?"

"Primitive. That's the word, all right, Plangman."

"Tub Oakley's favorite word for me. 'Harvey,' he used to say, 'you're a nice fellow, but you're so primitive.' I hated

it when he said that. It was just a remark to him, but I
hated it, and I kept remembering it.... Well, sir? Do you
want to go over the details?"

"I don't have the money." Yet, oddly enough, as he said
that, Bowser did not feel that he distrusted Plangman any
longer. Plangman was too vulnerable. Bowser was stalling,
giving himself time to think. São Paulo seemed a very long
way off, and Bowser had the same feeling he had had
earlier that evening in his study—that it was too big a
jump—from here to there. Perhaps just this sort of person
was the right one for now, just this sort of cockeyed plan—
as unlikely as any Bowser could ever be a part of, and for
that reason, good. And it was a gamble—but with someone
like Plangman, the odds were in favor of Robert Bowser.
Bowser felt sure of that. Plangman would always be more
off guard than Bowser. The $10,000 was cheap enough a
price for time, and a place to hide.

"You'll get the money, sir," Plangman was saying. "You
see, I'll tell my mother you're a professor I met—that you're
on a leave of absence, to write a thesis. I'll tell her that in
return for a place to stay, you agree to look after 702. As
I mentioned earlier, the house is in fairly good condition,
sir. We've converted it into three apartments. You'll live in
mine, on the first floor, as I said. The other two are rented."

"In this fantasy of yours, Mr. Plangman," Bowser said,
"what do you plan to do?"

"I'm going to get an apartment in New York, sir. A very
swanky one. I'll invent some sort of business I'm supposed
to be in. You can help me with that. I'll need to be sure
of myself around Mr. Cutler. Weekends I'll spend around
here, seeing Lois. I thought of moving here, but I know
how important it is to play it cool, sir. I just need time
and the trappings, Mr. Bowser. A nice place. A nice car.
Some advice. I'll write you for advice. I'll need a lot. I
hope you're a good correspondent. Then, there's a European
trip in the offing. I want either to stall it, or be included.
I wouldn't mind going to Europe on my honeymoon."

"How would you explain to the Cutlers your sudden
shortage of funds? Ten thousand doesn't stretch far, Plangman." Bowser was thinking that he would be well out of
the whole situation before Plangman went through the money.
Time was all he needed. If he had had more warning
from the beginning, would he have chosen São Paulo? Probably not. It would not be his meat at all, doing his sort of

work in a country whose language he could not speak. Canada was more likely.

"I'll explain it some way," said Plangman. "A bad investment, a business loss. I'll need your advice on that too. The important thing is to win over Hayden Cutler—to endear myself to him, sir. I'll honestly need a lot of advice."

God, what a fool he really was! Half of Bowser pitied him, and the rest scorned him and his kind.

Bowser said, "Who advised you how to go about blackmailing?"

"I saw my chance and I took it, Mr. Bowser, the same as you saw your chance to become an embezzler, and became one. We're quite a lot alike, Mr. Bowser. Do you realize that?"

"Oh, certainly, Plangman, certainly!" Bowser laughed inside; oh great god, what a fool!

"Do you come here often, sir?"

"I've never been here before."

"Good, sir. I'm glad to hear that. It may work in our favor, that you're not remembered as we sit here. What was I saying? Oh . . . that we're alike. Yes, sir. You're as much a victim of your way of life as I am of mine. It's too bad you never wanted out, as I did. It's too bad you never dreamed of entering my world, as I have of entering yours. Wouldn't everything be perfect then! Oh, by the by, sir, I'll want your passport. I don't want to take the chance of your leaving me. I want your passport and the $10,000 before we part tonight. We can do it anyway you want. We can go to your house together, or I can park just down the road and you can bring them out to me. Do you think we should chance being seen together by your wife and mother-in-law? Once the authorities discover your theft, sir, they'll be questioning anyone who's had anything to do with you. Of course, we can always explain the wallet mix-up—but I don't know that I should be hanging around your house. They might look into my background a bit more. I wouldn't want them to go to 702 Wentwroth, would you?"

"Supposing I were to go along with you, Plangman," said Bowser, "why do you want me to go to Columbia, Missouri? Why do you insist on this business of my living in your place? I could live anywhere just as well, and advise you, couldn't I?"

Harvey Plangman said, "Well, for one thing—someone has to take care of the house. Summer session is almost over now. There'll be two new tenants in the fall. I'd either have to pay someone to look after the place, or do it myself. I haven't got time to scout around for someone, and I haven't time to spend in Columbia. You appreciate that. For another thing—it's the safest place for you, I feel. If you were to get caught, I'd very likely have to give back the money. I'd be an accessory, in fact. So your safety is important, don't you see?"

"I could run out on you in Missouri. You've thought of that, I suppose." Bowser was curious now, to see just how far ahead Plangman had thought.

"Yes, but why should you? Safety is important to you too. Sunday night we'll fly to Columbia together. I'll introduce you to mother and take you over to 702 and get you settled. Then I'll fly back East, after I've done some packing. If you skip out then, an anonymous phone call to the police would probably put them onto you in a matter of days— even hours. They'd know your jumping-off point, anyway. But you won't run out on me. The heat will be on, you know."

Robert Bowser weighed it all over carefully. It might even be a godsend, and not a gamble at all. It just might be a godsend.

Plangman clapped his hand across his shoulder. "It could be so much worse, don't you see that? You could be in handcuffs now."

"If you were to turn the letter over to the police, do you think they'd believe you? I could say I'd never written it."

"Why do you still fight me, sir? In the first place, I'd probably take the letter to someone like Hayden Cutler— explain the jacket mix-up and all, and let him act. He'd carry more authority, wouldn't you say? Of course, before I did that, I'd probably read it to your wife over the phone. She already knows about the jacket mix-up. I wonder what she'd say to the letter, hmmm? Ah, but, sir, let's get on with our plan."

"And do you keep the letter?"

"Of course not, sir. I'm a very fair person. I thought we'd mail it to your wife Sunday night, before we get our plane to Missouri. That way, I can make sure you don't change your mind. From now, until the time Mrs. Bowser receives the letter, it'll be our special secret. It's interesting, isn't it, that 24 hours ago we'd never even heard of one another— and now, our lives have been changed completely around by each other. Driving here tonight, I tried to think what really caused this. I thought—for my own part—it's almost a gift from the gods. It's almost as though they looked down and saw me being humiliated again, and they said to themselves, all right—okay, let's throw a break that fellow's way. Let's see what he can do with one decent break. It might have been a gift from the gods in your case too, sir, though it'd never occur to you. We never know. But I believe there's a reason that it was you, in particular, and me, in particular —us, in particular, sir. I believe that."

"Why $10,000, Plangman? Why did you decide on that amount?"

"I think you have about $50,000, sir. I don't know why I think that, and I probably underestimate it—but there you are. And I'm not greedy. And I like you, sir. I honestly like you. You could be my father, you know."

"Suppose I told you I had only $12,000 to my name. You wouldn't believe that, I gather?"

"I might. I'd still need ten."

"What would you expect me to live on?"

"On the rent from 702, sir, just as I would have. It comes to $200 a month. If you want to do the superintendent work as well, there'll be a little extra from Mother."

"You have it all worked out, hmm?"

"Yes. It all began to fall together like pieces in a puzzle —like pieces simply assembling themselves. I hardly heard a word Lois said tonight, sir. I just kept trying your number . . . shouldn't we go now, sir?"

"Wait . . . wait . . . I have to think."

"Yes . . . you see, sir, anything that's defective in my plans, you must call to my attention As I say, it all fell together like a puzzle being solved, but there could be mistakes. It's time for you to do some thinking now. Does your wife know my name, for example?"

"I don't know. The police will question you, if Margaret does remember your name. They may question you anyway—someone could have seen us together tonight."

"Well, sir, when I have dinner at the Cutlers, I'll mention that our wallets became crossed—that we picked up each other's coat by mistake. If the police do question me eventually, they'll corroborate my story."

"No, don't do that."

"No?"

"No, because I'm not sure Margaret knows your name.

I can't remember her saying it at any point. I didn't even mention that you were from Columbia, Missouri. I think I simply said Missouri. It's better to stay uninvolved, unless you can't help it."

"All right, I won't mention it. I haven't mentioned a thing to Lois. That was lucky."

"Yes . . . I do have to do something about my glasses." As Robert Bowser talked, he felt the beginnings of a slight euphoria; it was good to be able to talk about it, a relief. "There's a place with three hour service on lower Broadway, I think."

"I'm glad you see things my way, sir. I mean it when I say that I like you. I wish you liked me . . . never mind . . . I wouldn't want to turn you in sir, honestly."

"The haircut. Maybe at the airport, just before we leave."

"On Sunday night, sir? They won't be open. We'll stay over in St. Louis when we arrive. You can get the haircut there, Monday morning. That way you'll go to Columbia looking like the new Robert Bowser. Yes, and you'll have to think of a new name, sir. I envy you! Harvey Plangman! I'd give anything to change my name."

"I'll keep the same initials . . . some of my things are monogrammed. My luggage is . . . A handkerchief or two . . . shirts."

"Mr. Bowser, I wouldn't pack a large bag, sir. You'll want to dress differently. I'll give you pointers, sir. Maybe some of my old things will suit you. The professors around Missouri are rather seedy, on the whole. You know, sir— tweed jackets with leather elbow patches, corduroy jackets, charcoal slacks—a cap might be just right too."

"Don't come to the house. You can park down the road, with your lights out. I'll meet you there."

"Sir?"

"What?"

"I have to leave the car I'm driving in New York to-morrow. As you know I'm having dinner at the Cutlers to-morrow night. I thought you'd give me some advice. Maybe when I'm in New York I'll buy something special for the Cutlers' dinner, like a Garbieri Canterbury belt. What would you say to that?"

"*What?*"

"Sir, if I make mistakes—if I say things that seem out-landish to you, I'd appreciate it if you wouldn't wince like that."

"What's a Garbieri Canterbury belt?"

"I'm just surprised you don't know, sir. It's a very expensive belt. I don't see anything odd about wanting one. I'm just surprised you don't know of it, sir."

"We'd better get the check."

"Yes . . . he sees us . . . he'll bring it. Another thing, sir. When you pack . . . if you have any ties . . . good ones . . . you know? You won't have much use for them, and I—I could use them."

"Are you having dinner at the Cutlers tomorrow night?"

"Sir, I've been telling you that all along."

"Not in that shirt, I hope—nor in those trousers. You look just—oh well," Bowser sighed, frowning.

"What would you suggest, Mr. Bowser?" Harvey Plangman smiled, leaning forward.

TEN

Dear Mr. B.,

Mother writes that you are a real find. I couldn't agree more. She says you had an eye infection when she stopped by last week. The contact lenses? It's important, I think, that you learn to wear them and do without the glasses altogether. When you wear glasses, there's still a trace of Robert Bowser in your looks, and now with fall coming, the campus will be crowded with all sorts of people—some who might have a good memory. Fortunately, though, I've seen no photographs of you in current papers. I wouldn't mention the fact that you're breaking in contact lenses either—it's too suspicious for a man your age. People will wonder.

In Bucks County you are a man of mystery. Conversation almost verbatim last p.m. with Hayden Cutler.

Me-What are the newest theories on that Bower fellow who embezzled the money?—(Note the Bower—ha! ha!)
H.C.-You mean Bowser. Robert Bowser, I never knew him, of course, but since the whole thing became public information, I've heard quite a lot about him. Odette knew him. She runs one of our local restaurants. She—everyone, for that matter, says he simply wasn't the type to embezzle money. Most people favor the theory he was under some outside pressure. Then, there was this peculiar business of the strange man who met him at the gas station in Lambertville, a night or so before his disappearance.
Me-Yes, I seem to remember something about a stranger appearing suddenly from nowhere.

H.C.-I doubt that he was a stranger to Robert Bowser.
     He probably had something on him, you know.
     He'd probably been black-mailing him for years.
 Me-What could he have on him, though?
H.C.-His wife keeps insisting there couldn't be another
     woman involved. Men like Bowser are often just the
     type to tangle with some frowzy sort of female.
 Me-What do you mean 'men like Bowser'? What was
     he like?
H.C.-The mousy type, from all I hear.

Well, "mousy", there you are. (No offense, sir. A joke
is a joke.)

I drove by your house when I left the Cutlers. All is
serene. No one seemed to be moving out or moving in.
Life seems to go on without you.

Now, for my life.

It is strangely uncomplicated. Do you know that Hayden Cutler hasn't questioned me at all about myself?
Certainly not the way I expected he would. After his
initial remark about never having heard of a Colonel
Plangman, he's made no inquiries about my family.
I didn't even get a chance to use that story we con-
cocted about my father's secret work with Rand Corporation. You were right—he knows nothing about this
government agency. I would have been perfectly safe
mentioning it. I did mumble something about my father
working for Rand, and he said, "Remington Rand?"
"Oh, no, sir," said I, "It's Research and Development.
My father was connected with research for their program with the United States Air Force." Then I looked
very closely into his eyes (you know the way I do)
and I said, "I'm surprised you never heard of them,"
That, sir, was the end of that.

You are quite right. I am safer sticking to academic or
intellectual-type allusions. When I told him I was studying for my doctor's degree at Columbia, he said his
brother Avery was the "brain" in their family. He said
Avery finally came to his senses and went into business. That was a good opening for me. I said, "More

and more I've been wondering if I really want to teach. .... I like the business world myself." Well, sir, there was no job offer or anything like that, but slowly I plant my little seeds.

I took the bus up to Columbia and looked around— just in case I ever have to answer questions about the campus. I got a catalog of courses listed for their graduate school of journalism too. You were right. It seems logical that I would go from Missouri school of journalism to a graduate school. I explained to Cutler that I thought of going to Princeton for my undergraduate work, but with a school of journalism right in my own back yard, so to speak (said I) it seemed pointless to attend a college that did not offer the subjects I was interested in.

Oddly enough, my problem seems not to be Mr. Cutler, but Lois. I know she's fond of me. It's just that it's very hard to get her mind off him, for very long.

Next Saturday they are both coming to dinner at my place. He's a great eater. I'd love to have something simple to fix, yet special. Could you suggest something? Something very chic. Can you think of anything?

The European trip is still being discussed between them. I must make more headway. The thing is, I wonder if either one is taking me seriously. Oh, don't worry, sir, I'm sure they are. It's just an aside. I'm actually doing very, very well! Yesterday I bought an under-the-knot-design silk tie in light gray (Countess· Mara) and for my desk an initial paperweight in rich Florentine gold finish, initial P, naturally. It looks very handsome. I expect to leave it on top my desk when they come to dinner. I like the Countess Mara ties because they have the little crown and the C.M. on them, and everyone knows (who knows anything at all) that it's a good tie.

Well, sir, that's my news.

Do you like being Raymond Battle? I know you won't

answer that, since your letters seem unfriendly and
impersonal. You seem interested only in answering my
questions as succinctly as possible and being done
with me until you write again. I'm not criticising you,
by any means. It's just a remark. By the by, Hayden
Cutler happened to know what a Garbieri Canterbury
belt is. I bought one and wore it last week, and when
I said, "This is a Garbieri Canterbury belt I'm wearing." he said, "Oh, yes. Indeed." You just smirked,
remember? Bygones are bygones, though.

Sincerely yours, Harvey.

Raymond Battle ripped the letter to shreds and dropped
it down the toilet. He blinked tears away, tears that came
whenever he had to look at anything closely—then wiped
under his eyes with a piece of Kleenex, being careful not
to disturb the lenses. He looked in the mirror. His eyes no
longer became bloodshot when he wore the lenses, but
there was a certain glassiness to his expression, very much as
though he were slightly dazed or gone a little soft in the
head. Nevertheless, his appearance was remarkably changed.
His hair was cropped very close to his head, and he had
grown a small Hitlerish mustache. He had taken up pipe-
smoking, and he had taken to wearing a cap about, both in-
doors and out—a sort of baseball cap. His usual costume was
a pair of comfortable khaki pants, a checkered sports shirt,
ankle-high dirty white sneaks with heavy cotton socks—and
on cool evenings, a black cotton coat sweater. He was no
surprise to anyone at 702 Wentwroth, who called on him
to fix a fuse or let water out of a radiator. He had rejected
Harvey's idea to pose as a professor working on his thesis,
out of a fear that he might accidentally be pulled into academic circles. Instead, Raymond Battle was simply a for-
mer high school teacher, who had lost his wife suddenly.
It was this story which Harvey told his mother—that Raymond
Battle, suffering an immense bereavement, needed to escape
memories of his wife—that he needed to get a hold on
himself—perhaps to write a novel he had been planning.

In apartment 3 at 702, was a young widow. She was a redhead in her twenties, with two children. Mrs. Plangman had
told her Raymond Battle's sad story, and she had come down
for a look at Raymond, almost the same day she had settled in. There was no threat of involvement from that source;

she had glanced up and down at Raymond, while rattling on about the hall light and a stopper for their bathtub, and her round blue eyes had very noticeably not widened, nor had she wasted any smiles on Raymond Battle. She was studying dramatics at the University and her mother lived with her. The mother had been in vaudeville at one time; she wore tapered slacks and tight sweaters, with high heels and lots of bracelets clanking on her wrist. Her hair was bleached platinum, and afternoons while her daughter went to classes, Raymond could hear Mrs. Hill coaching her grandchildren in songs like "Bye, Bye Blackbird" and "Toot-Toot-Tootsie."

Apartment 2 housed Professor Bullard, a Shakespeare scholar, who kept very much to himself, except when there was no hot water. Then he would slap down the stairs in his bedroom slippers to complain.

Raymond Battle did feel safe there. There was more to it than that; he liked it there. He liked fixing things. It amazed him whenever he could repair something, make something work again. He found he had a knack for it, and it gave him a peculiar sensation of delight which was way out of proportion to the simple accomplishment. Everything he did had its exaggerated sense of pleasure. He developed little rituals and routines, like a very old man who has lived alone for a long, long time. In the early morning when he rose, he timed his tea to be ready at the exact moment he finished buttering a piece of toast, and there was a particular table he set out his teacup on, a special chair he pulled up to it—and always when he brought his breakfast into the room where he ate it, he remembered to place his paper napkin under the plate of toast he carried. He never had to make more than one trip from the kitchen.

At night, when he undressed for bed, he hung his khaki's over the chair, and placed his sneakers under it. Then he put his shirt around the chair's shoulders—and there was the chair, more or less containing him, and it was all so simple. He slept naked. He had never done that before, either. He had never even walked around naked before, and somehow he enjoyed doing it—it was a part of his new freedom. There were times when he ate spaghetti cold from the can; it was his first taste of canned spaghetti, or canned beans, or canned chili. It tasted good to him. He became pleased at the fact his food bills per week were very low, and he was eating well—getting plenty down. Working around 702 gave him a different sort of appetite—a sudden, overwhelming hunger that never would have waited out before-dinner cocktails, or polite napkin straightening. He gulped his food down, sometimes standing up in the kitchen—sometimes setting himself a place at the card table he set up there. But always, he gulped his big meal of the day—and afterwards he knew he had eaten. He felt the gratification of his body as it received the food and put it to use—another feeling that had never been there.

For diversion, Raymond Battle went to the movies sometimes. He found himself dividing his time between movies and television. He would notice what pictures were coming to the theaters in town, and how long they were playing—and then he would decide which night would be the best to see the pictures, without giving up something good on television. He particularly liked audience participation shows, or shows that re-enacted someone's real life. He would choke up a bit when some brother from Cork County, Ireland, was reunited with a sister from Jersey City, after twenty-five years. Or when a poor fellow whose house had burned to the ground was marched up from the audience and presented with a full year's rent in a new house, and a freezer filled with frozen dinners for his family of six. He kept the sound low and the windows closed when he watched those shows, and he watched all he could, often taking an hour off here and there during the day, when many of them were on. Sundays when he got the papers, he often looked at the television page immediately, and planned his week's watching, going through the Monday—Saturday listings with a warm sense of anticipation. Occasionally he took a pencil and circled out his week's TV watching.

One of the things he liked best was marketing at the A&P in town. He worked it so that he would only have one large paper bag to carry on the bus, but he spent hours inside the store, wandering from display to display, picking out new products, and selecting or rejecting products he had seen advertised on television. He was meticulous about that, punishing those manufacturers whose commercials were bad, and rewarding those whose commercials were good. When he came upon products whose companies he knew well, such as Baker Oats, he was faithful to them too. Sometimes, after one of these expeditions to town, while he rode the bus home, he would momentarily start dwelling on the food bills Robert Bowser had paid. He was not even sure of the amounts. Margaret had handled that. But he had a rough idea—a sure knowledge that they had been preposterously large. Instead of anger, he felt only a terrible confusion, as though all of it had nothing to do with him any more, and yet there you were—it had everything to do with him. Immediately following that thought was the thought that now he was simply going through the motions of living, waiting for a real thing to happen—marking time—this wasn't real. A fearful loneliness overtook him then. He wanted to talk to somebody, anybody. Not about himself—just to talk, and listen, and talk—with somebody. Usually he would write Harvey Plangman on those nights after he got home. Sometimes he would write very elaborate letters telling everything he had done, what he had seen at the movies or on TV, and say what he thought about it all. But he always ripped them up, and sent, instead, a very terse note answering Harvey's latest questions.

There were times when he talked to himself aloud. Never very loud. He was a little embarrassed when he did it, and always aware he was doing it. Usually he ended with a silly little chuckle, as though he knew he were foolish—as though he knew, and anyone listening would know he knew. But of course there was no one listening. He never would have chanced it, if there were that possibility.

That morning, after he ripped up Harvey's newest letter and flushed it down the toilet, he said to himself, "The little crown and the C.M.! The little crown and the C.M.!" His chuckle was sarcastic, superior. Then he jumped. He heard a voice from the next room.

He called, "Hello, who is it?"

"Mrs. Hill, Mr. Battle. I've been knocking on your door. I didn't know if you were in or out, so I just tried the handle."

"I'll be right out."

"I'm sorry if you were in the bathroom."

Mrs. Hill was wearing tight violet pedal-pushers and a tight lemon-colored sweater. On her feet were over-sized white furry slippers, and she was carrying a long cigarette holder, with a cigarette burned down nearly to the end. She gave Raymond Battle one of her quick, prefatory smiles and launched in. "You're such a nice man, Mr. Battle. I couldn't come to many men with this sort of problem. But you're such a nice man! My daughter and I often mention that fact. I'd trust you with anything I had, though the good Lord knows

that isn't much these days. I hope I didn't get you out of the
bathroom ... the thing is, Mr. Battle, I'm supposed to go into
St. Louis tonight and stay over, and my daughter's trying out
for The Corn Is Green, over at the University. The thing is,
Mr. Battle, we called three sitters and they're all booked."

"Baby-sitters, Mrs. Hill?"

"My daughter's not going out until eight and she'll be back
before midnight. If the kids miss their naps this afternoon,
they'll be sound asleep in their beds at eight, Mr. Battle."

"I see ... you want me to sit."

"Would you, Mr. Battle? Believe me, we'd never ask you
again; it's just this once."

"Once, I suppose. I suppose I could once."

Mrs. Hill bounced across the room and planted a kiss on
his cheek. "Oh, God love you, Mr. Battle!" she said.

When she banged out the door and up the steps of 702,
Raymond Battle touched his cheek, moist from her lips. He
realized it was Raymond Battle's first kiss. There was the aroma
left from her perfume, an irritating spicy odor of some cheap
scent. He felt a sudden slow aching inside that was not desire,
that was not revulsion either—but that gave him a very
fleeting vision of a pale blue chiffon scarf whipping in the
wind, against a creamy summer crêpe dress and the glint of
the large gold Jay Thorpe necklace in the sun.

"Balenciaga's Quadrille?" the familiar voice said, "I wear
Quadrille most of the time."

He looked down at the rug and saw a long cigarette ash
which had dropped from Mrs. Hill's holder. He took his foot
and ground the ash into the rug, thinking, this isn't like
you at all, Robert.

Aloud he murmured, "You know me pretty well, don't
you?"

But he didn't miss Margaret; it was himself he missed.

ELEVEN

It was good to be waiting for someone. Harvey Plang-man did not even care that Boy was already ten minutes late. Harvey sat at a corner table in the Plaza bar, shuffling through his Speak Easy Pocket Language cards.

He was learning German. He was enrolled in a course for beginners at the New School down on 12th Street in New York City. The class was a disappointment. He had hoped to meet people, to make a friend or two whom he could meet for coffee on an afternoon, or drinks some evening; someone to invite up to his apartment, or some-one with whom to go to the movies, or the theater. He found that after class everyone hurried off, everyone seemed to have a date, and before class, they all sat with their heads buried in their books, going over their lessons before Frau Browder arrived. In addition, Harvey was not learning the language as rapidly as the others were. He made mistakes when he was called on, and he had purposely missed last even-ing's session to spare himself the embarrassment of not having his lesson prepared. With the Speak Easy Pocket Language Cards he bought at Brentano's book store that afternoon he might very well drop out of that course at the New School and learn German on his own. Why should he be humiliated every Tuesday and Thursday evening; humiliated and then left out after class, while all the others went their separate ways?

He had not enrolled in the course just to meet people. He wanted to have a second language, the same way Lois had French. Lois corresponded with a man who was in Europe, and the whole correspondence was in French. "He's just a friend," Lois always said about him, but it galled Harvey that they wrote back and forth in a foreign language; it made it intimate, somehow, and special. French was out of the question, since he could never hope to catch up with Lois. She knew no German. Already in his conversations with her, he was able to throw in snatches of the language. "Ah, guten abend!" he would greet her—

and one evening he had purposely chosen a restaurant in Yorkville to take her to, so he could tell the waiter, "Ich möchte gern einen dry martini, sehr kalt, bitte."

He was not seeing as much of Lois as he had hoped. It was a simple matter for her to drive into New York with her father any morning, and return with him in the evening. She had her own car as well. And Harvey had purchased an MG, like the one he had driven East for Tucker Wolfe. (He had told Lois that he had traded his old MG for a new one.) There was no lack of transportation. When Harvey offered to drive to New Hope and get her, she insisted that she would not let him do that—it was too far, back and forth. She was afraid to take her own car, because of the New York City traffic. As for driving in with her father, her answer was, "But what would I do all day while you were in class, Harvey?"

"I'll take the day off," Harvey would tell her.

"But what would we do all day?"

Harvey had no answer to that. Somehow he had never anticipated the question. He had thought Lois would know dozens and dozens of people in New York. He had imagined them rushing about in taxis, seeing this one and that, squeezing in a matinee here, a concert there—a trip to a museum —cocktails—lunches. Once he had bought tickets to *Sail Away* for a Wednesday matinee. Lois had driven in with her father, arriving at Harvey's apartment at ten-thirty in the morning. Harvey's place was a sublet, complete with a record collection and hi-fi, off Fifth in the eighties. He had *Carmen* turned up very loud when Lois rang his bell, and over his trousers and shirt (with a handsome Countess Mara tie) he was wearing his new bright red Oriental-style Sulka Luxury Lounging Robe. On his feet were his new double-duty soft leather slippers from Fellman Ltd., and he had incense burning in a special holder he had purchased at Bonnier's. They had cup of coffee after cup of coffee before Lois said the one opera she most detested was *Carmen* (Daddy agrees! Daddy calls it Carminative!) and that the incense was making her sick to her stomach. Neither one was hungry at lunchtime, but Harvey had reservations at Sardi's and they went there. They were herded upstairs, where Lois claimed all tourists were sent, and during lunch they both brooded to themselves and picked at Caesar salads. Harvey, who had imagined a much different luncheon mood (dazzled by the Sulka robe and the elegant setting and the wild, hot music, she had given herself to him and was still stirred by his prowess; they were holding hands under the table) noticed for the first time that her hair was not golden, it was the color of broken egg yolk, and her lipstick did not follow the line of her lips, but widened to the skin around her mouth, so that literally her mouth was painted on her face. After the theater, the hours before she was to meet her father to return to Bucks County were years long. She did not particularly want a cocktail, and it was raining so that they could not kill time walking about. While Harvey had three Scotches at the Algonquin, Lois Cutler sat beside him ripping paper napkins to shreds and breaking swizzle sticks in half. Harvey had the horrible notion that the whole thing was finished then and there, that disenchantment had been poured down on Lois like dirty dishwater from an upper story window. He blamed her for not having gay, smiling friends they might have gone to see together—and the old feeling came back that she did have them, probably, but she would not call on them with Harvey Plangman.

His comeback was spectacular. A week later he called Lois and suggested a little surprise birthday party for her father. The two of them took Daddy to Odette's for dinner. Harvey had arranged for a huge cake, for the piano player to burst into Happy Birthday as the cake was served, and for the lights to dim, and everyone to sing. He had paid for the whole evening, and Lois had kissed him very passionately in the parking lot ouside, afterwards, and told him it was the nicest thing she had ever heard of anyone doing. It was the first night he had been invited to stay over at the Cutlers. Again, he had hoped Lois would express her appreciation in emphatic physical display, and again, Lois had resisted what Harvey was sure, by now, must be a temptation to her.

Meeting Boy Ames quite accidentally on Fifth Avenue last week was a stroke of luck. Harvey had heard that Boy had transferred from Missouri, but he had not known Boy was living right down the block on Park Avenue, that he had dropped out of college altogether. In their brief conversation, Boy did not say he had left school for financial reasons, but Harvey believed that was the reason. His father's death had caused a drain on the family's finances, Harvey suspected, never mind the Park Avenue address.

There were plenty of people with the same address, struggling to afford it.

Harvey had told Boy nothing of his own doings, simply that he had an apartment a short way from where they had stopped to talk. They had agreed to look up one another very soon. Harvey had gone home feeling gay and clever, planning a future that now included Boy. Since they were neighbors, they would see one another—occasionally, in the beginning—by accident, as they had that day. Harvey would have Boy around for drinks. Boy would be able to see immediately that Harvey was a new person. Then too, Boy's own predicament would make him more sympathetic to Harvey. Neither one of them would ever be college graduates. Harvey would make up for all the Kappa Pi's who had probably dropped Boy by now, or simply forgotten him. Harvey would demonstrate true loyalty; he would even offer to lend Boy money, if Boy needed it. Eventually, if things worked well, Harvey would confide in Boy—ask his advice. Harvey was tired of Bowser's advice. He would like to write Bowser and tell him he no longer needed advice. He imagined Bowser's anxieties at such news, imagined a worried letter from Bowser. (That doesn't mean you're going to turn me in, does it? Please don't.) He imagined Boy and Lois and himself out on the town one night, night clubbing and laughing in the purple beginnings of dawn, whistling for cabs, all a little high, with Lois snuggling up to him.

"Do you like Boy?" he would say.

"Oh, yes! He's great fun! And I love you!"

He imagined them, whipping down Park in a cab singing "We Three" at the top of their lungs, all in evening dress, bound for nightcaps at Harvey's place. Lois would stay over.

As it turned out, Boy and he did not meet by accident after their initial meeting. Several times, Harvey walked along Fifth at the same hour he had first encountered him, and several times he walked by Boy's apartment building, around six p.m., when he imagined Boy would be returning from work. He was not sure where Boy worked; he hoped it was someplace that would not embarrass him. Four days passed, and finally Harvey called Boy. He asked him to drop over to the apartment, but Boy said he was tied up that night. They had agreed to meet this night, at the Oak Room in the Plaza, at nine-thirty.

The first thing Boy said when he joined Harvey at the

table was not, "I'm sorry I'm late." (Harvey had planned to say back, "That's all right, I was late myself.")

Boy said instead, "Good God, are you wearing perfume, Plangman?"

"It's 'Pour Un Homme'."

"What the hell is that?"

"Men's cologne. Pour un Homme—for a man."

"Smells more like it's for a fruity man. I hope you haven't gone that way."

"It's a very expensive French product," said Harvey. "I'm surprised you haven't heard of it, Boy."

Boy Ames shrugged and lit a cigarette. Harvey had not expected things to begin this way; it threw him off. He put his Speak Easy Pocket Language Cards back in his coat and stared glumly down at the ashtray. Boy signaled the waiter and ordered a Seven-Up.

"Aren't you drinking?" said Harvey.

"Too soon after dinner."

Harvey had imagined them both getting a little high together, a little confidential.

"I just had dinner a while ago myself," he said, "but I'm having some Old Smuggler and water."

"I'm having Seven-Up," said Boy. "How's Mom Plangman?"

"Oh, fine, fine. How are you, Boy? How are you making out?"

"I'm doing okay."

"Really?"

"We've been pretty busy these last few days. There was a news leak on rising soybean prices that had us jumping."

"Soybeans?"

"I'm with the New York Mercantile Exchange."

"I see," Harvey lied.

"You know, it's a commodity exchange. Soybeans, eggs, grain, potatoes. Commodities is the rage now, and I wish it weren't. Less work for old Boysey when it's quieter."

"It's too bad about your not finishing college, Boy. I know how you feel."

"I miss the old KP's, but I was wasting my time back there. Say, I saw Lake Budde the other night. He said he'd seen you during the summer. Didn't you drive Tucker's car East or something?"

"That was a long time ago."

"Lake said it was July, wasn't it? June or July?"

"No," Harvey said, "what I mean is, a lot has happened since then. I'm living here in New York now."

"So you said the other day. What are you doing?"

"Business. It's a deal I'm working on."

"You were always a hustler, Plangman."

The waiter brought Boy's drink and he raised it in a salute to Harvey. "Cheers!"

"Sursum corda!" said Harvey.

"What the hell does that mean?"

"It means 'Lift up your hearts!' It's Latin."

"You beat all, Plangman!" Boy Ames chuckled.

"What do you mean by that?"

"Nothing, buddy, nothing! Tell me about your new business deal."

Harvey said, "It's very strange the way I'm treated by both you and Lake. You seem to say what the hell this and what the hell that, no matter what I do or say."

"C'mon, Harv, sursum corda!"

"What the hell am I wearing, and what the hell do I mean, and what the hell this and that. It's really very boring."

"Do I see red suspenders under your suit coat, Harv?"

"I suppose that's wrong too. For your information, Boy, I bought them at Schoenfeld's. They're red moire suspenders, and they sell matching garters with them."

"No kidding!" Boy Ames grinned. "Matching garters?"

"You know very well that if Lake Budde were sitting here telling you what I'm telling you, you'd listen."

"I'm listening, buddy."

"You're laughing at me."

"Same old Harvey."

"No," Harvey Plangman said, "I'm not the same old Harvey!"

"Okay, Plangman, okay—no need to raise our voices. Say, Lake said you were interested in some gal from Bucks County."

"Yes, yes, I am. She's a very nice girl."

"You know who I liked, Plangman? I liked that Gertrude you were shacking up with! Didn't she teach shorthand or something? Jesus, I remember how mad Mom P. was when you were carrying on with her over at your place. Mom P. used to get us boys in her suite and rant and rave about 'that woman'. Wasn't her name Gertrude?"

"She was trash," said Harvey Plangman. "She used to

write me very obscene notes. Every single one of them was oestrous."

"Was what?"

"Oestrous. It's a word referring to the oestrous cycle, the period of sexual heat."

Boy Ames threw back his head and roared. Harvey was not smiling. He felt blood rush to his cheeks and ears. Boy slapped his knee and said, "Oestrous! Jesus, I have to remember that!"

"I'm surprised you weren't familiar with the word."

"There were no Gertrudes in my life, buddy! Oestrous! Ha! Ha!"

"I'm glad I amuse you, Boy."

"Oh Jesus, oestrous! I wish some gal would write me a few oestrous notes!"

While Boy finished laughing and chuckling and sniffling, Harvey signaled to the waiter for another drink. While Boy was settling down, Harvey managed to say, "I'll probably be getting married soon."

"Really?"

"Yes. It's not definite of course. Did Lake tell you anything about her? I mentioned her to him."

"As a matter of fact, Plangman, we hardly discussed you. Lake was just in for a few hours Tuesday and we went down to Nick's to hear some Dixieland."

"Tuesday, Boy?"

"Last Tuesday."

"That was the night I wanted you to come for a drink at my place."

"Yeah, well, Lake was coming in."

Harvey said, "It seems to me you could have mentioned he was coming in. I would have invited both of you. We might all have gone to Nicks, mightn't we?"

"Sure, buddy. I just—didn't think of it, Plangman."

"That's quite all right. I'm used to it by now."

"Next time."

"Sure, next time. Next time!"

"Tell me about the gal you're marrying."

"Always next time. I'm used to it."

"Tell me about the gal you're marrying, Plangman."

"She's not a gal, Boy. I wish you'd show some respect. She's very prominent socially. Her father is on the exchange too, for your information. You may even know him. Hayden Cutler!"

"On the Mercantile Exchange?"

"On the Stock Exchange," Harvey said. "On the New York Stock Exchange!"

"Good for him."

"I don't know if the Mercantile Exchange is more important than the New York Stock Exchange, but her maternal grandparents were descended from John Alden and Henry Adams."

Again, Boy burst into laughter. "Oh Jesus, I do remember Lake telling me something about that. I remember the John Alden, Henry Adams bit——ha! ha!"

"It's true! It's a true story!"

Boy was rocking back and forth in his chair, his face very red from laughing.

"Her uncle's a Boocock!" Harvey said angrily.

"Boocock, Plangman! Jesus, but that sounds oestrous!"

Harvey picked up his drink and gulped it down. He could feel his heart banging against his new S.A. Avery narrow-pleated shirt. He signaled the waiter for another drink, his hands trembling with humiliation.

It was eleven-fifteen when Harvey Plangman arrived back at his apartment. He was quite drunk. He had gulped his last three, and his very last he had been forced to drink by himself. Boy had said he had a date downtown, when Harvey suggested Boy wait, so they could cab home together. Boy had said he would give Harvey a ring one day soon. Harvey never wanted to see Boy Ames again. The whole episode had failed miserably. At one point Boy had laughed so hard, tears had run down his cheeks and he had said his stomach hurt from laughing. Harvey had forced him to be serious only once, at a point when Harvey spoke of Boy's father's death. Harvey had begun to be high at that point and he had asked Boy just exactly how Lake had broken the news to Boy.

"Just exactly what did Lake Budde say," Harvey had asked. "I'm just curious."

Boy Ames had answered. "You don't remember things like that in terms of exact words, Plangman, but Lake handled it just great! Lake," Boy Ames said solemnly, "is a beautiful person!"

A beautiful person—as Harvey stumbled around his apartment, getting out of his clothes, fixing himself a nightcap, and wrapping himself in his red Sulka dressing gown, he

kept thinking back on those three words. Boy made them
sound so spiritual, so damned special—the way Boy had
said them, they no longer seemed like ordinary, everyday
words—the combination of them and Boy's tone, made them
seem as though they had never been spoken before. A
beautiful person. Harvey liked it. He wished someone would
say that about him; he wished there were someone he
could say it about—just as Boy had said it. It was as though
they enhanced whoever said it, more than the person it was
said about.

Harvey sat down on the bed next to the telephone. Boy
had made him feel 100 times as left out as he felt after
his German classes. It was his lowest point since the change
in his life. It had put him back where he had been a year
ago, that far back, and he stared at the telephone as though
only that instrument could reinstate him now. The trouble
was, there was no one to call but Lois. With Lois, he had
never established a habit of casual chit-chat over the long
distance phone. Both of them were slightly self-conscious
on the telephone, and he had never called her without an
excuse for the call. He would have to think of an excuse. It
was eleven-twenty now, too. He would have to have a
reason for calling that late. On the bedtable was a stack of
cookbooks. He had spent that afternoon searching for a
recipe he might use for the dinner he was fixing Lois and
her father. One of the cookbooks was open to a recipe for
a pie, made of bottled gooseberries and scalded cream. Tears
came to his eyes as he looked at the recipe. Why was
everything in life so very complicated? Why did he need
to scald cream and make excuses to telephone the girl he
was planning to marry? Never mind. He was used to it. He
sat there afraid to shut his eyes because he would become
very dizzy, and he tried to make up an excuse. At last he
decided to say he was going out of town until Saturday—
that he would not return until late Saturday afternoon, and
that they had better decide on the dinner time this evening.

He lifted the phone's arm from its cradle and gave the
number to the operator.

"This is Harvey Plangman," he told Hayden Cutler. "I
hope it's not too late to call Lois."

"She's at the Playhouse," Cutler said. "Play's probably
over now. She ought to be home soon."

He wanted to keep Cutler on the phone, until he felt
reinstated. He would not be able to wait for Lois. He was

very, very tired, growing dizzy even without closing his eyes.

"I'm expecting you for dinner Saturday," he said.

"Yes."

"I'm fixing something special. Scalded cream."

"Pardon me?"

"Gooseberries with scalded cream," he said.

"Look, Harvey, Lois should be back in a half hour or so."

"Mr. Cutler?"

"Yes."

"Would it be better if I called her 'morrow morning?"

"I think it would."

" 'Morrow morning, first thing."

"All right, Harvey. I'll tell her you called."

"How are you?"

"Fine thanks. I'll tell Lois you'll call tomorrow."

"How're things at the Tock'change?"

"Just fine, Harvey."

"I hada drink Mercantile Exchange, Mr. Cutler. T'night."

"Yes, well, I think you'd better call tomorrow, Harvey."

"Mr. Cutler, sir?"

"Yes, Harvey!"

"Mr. Cutler, sir, you're a beautiful person."

There was a momentary pause, a click—and then the dial tone.

In his red Oriental-style Sulka Luxury Lounging Robe, Harvey Plangman spent the night passed out on the floor beside his bed, with all the lights burning.

TWELVE

RAYMOND BATTLE had arrived at Mrs. Carson's early. Her mother, Mrs. Hill, had gone hours ago to St. Louis, and the children, Chrissy and Carla, were already tucked in bed. It was quarter to eight by Raymond Battle's wristwatch. Time enough for a few amenities before Mrs. Carson left and Raymond began his chore of baby-sitting.

"Ah! You've added a desk up here, I see," said he, as young Mrs. Carson came from the bedroom to the living room. She was wearing a light blue skirt and a white sweater, with light blue Keds and no stockings. Her hair was a fiery red, and she had many freckles, a round sort of pretty baby-girl face, and a small but very well-developed figure. She certainly did not look like the mother of two children, but more like one of the new freshmen at the University. She was throwing things into a tan leather shoulder bag, murmuring to herself, ". . . my lipstick, my pencil, my compact, my saccharine, my hay fever pills . . ."

Again, Raymond Battle said, "You've added a desk up here, I see."

"It's all right, isn't it?" She took a wad of Kleenex from her bag and blew her nose, then rushed across to a table where a pair of pearl earrings were resting. Hurriedly, she screwed them on her lobes, saying, "It was my husband's mother's desk. It's a Governor Win-something. I don't remember. Not an original, natch."

"A Governor Winthrop," said Raymond Battle, wishing she would stand still for a moment and behave politely. After all, he was doing her a favor. He was certainly not going to accept payment for this chore.

He said, "These fall-front desks are called that. They're patterned after the fall-fronts from the Chippendale period, only their name is a misnomer."

She was nodding her head, but her attention was fixed on her change purse, which she was pushing through with her finger, counting to herself.

Raymond Battle walked closer and spoke louder, peeved

99

at her disinterest. She behaved like a spoiled child. "You see," he said, "although there were several governors named Winthrop, they all lived a good century before this type desk came into existence."

His voice, his nearness, had forced her to give him her attention. She fidgeted, looked at him with very vacant blue eyes.

He sighed and turned away, and she said, "The children should sleep right through, Mr. Battle. They didn't have naps this afternoon, natch."

He was slightly surprised at himself for remembering that little bit about eighteenth century furniture; he had really never been very interested. Everything he knew he had picked up from Margaret's talk, and he had always had the idea that he never listened to anything Margaret had to say on the subject—but there you were, he had. With such a good opportunity for conversation with a relative stranger, he was disappointed to find it thrust back at him, as though it were a boomerang, he had thrown out.

Mrs. Carson said, "Chrissy whimpers in her sleep. It doesn't mean anything. She's the baby, the two year-old."

Mrs. Carson was standing at the mirror in the living room now, fluffing up the sides of her short feather-cut hairdo with the palms of her hands. "There's some kind of wine there in the decanter on the table," she said. "I don't know what it is. I don't drink much. It's Mother's, but help yourself . . ."

"Oh, no, thank you," said Raymond Battle. "I'm going to write a letter. Probably watch television."

"Well, help yourself to anything you want."

"Thank you."

She turned around and their eyes met again. Her way of looking at him annoyed him—it was so much a way of not looking at him. He had no interest whatsoever in this person, and for that reason she irked him all the more—the very fact that she had imposed on him, and then could not even go through the simple social motions of attentive discourse or the gestures of a smile, or an expression of receptivity when he spoke. Before he knew it, she was out the door. Her footsteps on the stairs were every bit as self-concerned as she was, banging and important and rushing.

Raymond Battle was glad she was gone. His impulse earlier this afternoon, to talk with someone, was gone along with Mrs. Carson. There was no one worth talking with. On his way to Apartment 3, Battle had a brief encounter with Professor Bullard, who was going down the stairs as Battle was going up. They met on the landing. Raymond inquired, "And how are you, Professor?" to which the old man nodded, unsmiling—as seemed to be the custom at 702. Raymond had then said, "There's a runner loose on the stairs, about the third step. I'll fix it, but be careful as you go down." And Bullard's response? Not even waiting to hear the end of the sentence, Bullard clattered down the stairs reciting Shakespeare in a loud voice: "I am amaz'd, methinks, and lose my way, Among the thorns and dangers of this world." He bounced off the bottom step crying, "King John, Act Four!" He was out of the house without so much as a thank-you-for-the-warning to Raymond Battle.

Battle settled himself at the imitation Governor Winthrop, brought out his stationery box and ball point pen, and spread the equipment in front of him. He had an hour before the English mystery movie on television, and he lit his pipe (he was still new at it, still had difficulty keeping the pipe going) and began his letter.

Dear Plangman,

He sat back, gave four or five quick sucks on the pipe stem, then leaned forward and began with a determined air.

I am up here on 3, baby-sitting for a most annoying individual. I would guess she is no more than twenty-three or twenty-four—a redhead, with none of the volatile or tempestuous qualities redheads are alleged to have, but in their place, a vacantness. This is particularly evidenced by her way of looking at you. It's as though she's off somewhere in a very unexciting place. You know, of course, the expression "looking right through you." It's that. I suppose you would call her pretty; she has all the physical qualities that earn the adjective—but her inability to be present spiritually, at the same time her body is physically present, makes her more like some store window mannequin—worse, an animated one. One who says "natch!" for "naturally" and who suffers from hay fever and is dressed as a bobby-soxer. So much for that, I have already exaggerated her importance by devoting a paragraph to her.

You mention that you would like to serve the Cutlers something simple but unusual. Was "chic" the word you used? There's a very common Roman pasta dish which Margaret used to make occasionally on Thursday nights, way back in the beginning of our marriage. We had tasted the dish in Rome (it's everyday fare there) and Margaret had added a few improvisations of her own. I'll give it to you with her improvisations ... It's called spaghetti alla carbonara

1. Fry bacon while you are boiling the water for spaghetti.
2. To the bacon, after it is fried, add ground pepper and a few dashes of sage.
3. Place the cooked spaghetti (plain) on a plate. Add the bacon-sage mixture. On top of that add lots of grated Parmesan cheese.
4. Top with a raw egg yolk.
5. Serve as is, leaving it to the individual to stir it all together.

Serve it with a green salad and a bottle of red wine. I think ...."

At this point, Raymond Battle heard a banging in the bedroom. He dropped his pen and rushed into that room. He was confronted by the sight of the two year-old in her crib, on her knees, with her eyes closed, banging her head against the wooden headboard.

"Here, here," he said, bewildered and awkward, as he turned the child over on her back. "Go to sleep!" he said, ridiculously, because she was already fast asleep. Her thumb went to her mouth, and Raymond snapped off the overhead light, just as the child in the bed across the room from the crib, murmured "Nighty, Mum!"

Feebly, Raymond whispered, "Nighty."

He shut the door, uncertain about the whole thing. What on earth was the baby doing hitting her head against a wall! He had no idea, but somehow he thought of the silly redheaded person rushing off to a play rehearsal in blue sneakers, and he decided it had something to do with that. Perhaps the child was deranged.

Back at the desk in the living room, Raymond wadded up the letter to Plangman and tossed it in the wastebasket. On another piece of paper he simply wrote, "Dear Plangman, this a good recipe," copied down the recipe, and signed the letter: "R.B." He took an envelope from his stationery box, put a stamp on it, and shoved the paper inside.

Then he walked across the room and turned on the television.

He found he could not concentrate on the program which was finishing up, prior to the movie showing. He kept thinking of spaghetti alla carbonara—of that, and inevitably of the trip to Rome with Margaret years ago.

They had stayed at the Excelsior on the Via Vittorio Veneto. Long ago on trips they had learned to split up during the day and pursue their individual interests, meeting for cocktails in the evening. Margaret's interests were the same as they were in any city of the world. The beds in their hotel room would be stacked high at day's end with boxes from Fontana Arte, Myricae, Castelli, Buzzetti, Cartoni, and Bellini. Margaret would be both exhausted and exhilarated from her day of shopping, and Robert would be worried about paying for her purchases and tired from his own wanderings through museums and churches. It was not that Robert Bowser was unhappy about their periodic visits to Europe. He enjoyed them; he looked forward to them. But inevitably there was that corner of his thoughts which was wholly occupied with the dread knowledge he could not afford them. The incident Raymond Battle remembered, as he sat before the television set, was a strange little isolated one out of many, many trips as Robert Bowser, with spouse. They had met for cocktails that afternoon at the Fagianno, in the portico overlooking the famous column of Marcus Aurelius. He remembered that he was discussing the stoicism of that emperor with Margaret, going into the details of his reign, which was plagued by earthquakes and the attacks of Parthians, Germans and Britons—and he was at that point in Marcus Aurelius' life, when he was victor over the Marcomanni, when suddenly he noticed that Margaret was flirting with a man at the next table. He sat shocked, watching her. She had not even noticed that he had stopped talking. Her head was slightly tilted to one side, and she was alternately staring directly at the man and dropping her eyes for some slow seconds to her glass of Soave, only to lift them again and search the face of the man. The man looked very greasy to Robert Bowser, and hairy and too plump. He wore a cheap suit, and he needed a hair cut. He was smiling at Margaret, and Robert saw that his teeth were yellow and misshapen.

At last Robert said to her, "And just what is this little play all about?"

Margaret was very embarrassed. She said, "Don't be silly, Robert."

"It doesn't strike me that I'm the one who's silly."

"He's just a fool."

"I can see that," said Robert.

It was not jealousy that Robert felt at all. It was anger. Only moments before he had begun his discussion of the Roman Emperor, Margaret had confessed to the purchase of a very costly antique. Instead of losing control at this news—because they were on a holiday—and truthfully, Robert had to admit, because he was slightly afraid to go against Margaret when her mind was set, he had simply dropped the matter and turned to something more objective for discussion. He had felt very noble doing that, noble and husbandly, and thoughtful. Put-upon of course, but agreeable despite all. And there was Margaret leering at a greasy, yellow-toothed scoundrel, who doubtless could not even afford one of Margaret's hairdressing bills. And would never have to, what's more.

He remembered that he had sulked about it. Margaret teased him that he was jealous and she was pleased, and they said very little more until after dinner. Over some Strega, Robert remarked that the man was a very crude sort—that he was surprised at Margaret for letting down her barriers to such an extent—and in public.

Margaret retaliated by saying, "Sometimes we women can't be bought."

"What?" Robert had exclaimed.

"Sometimes," Margaret smiled to herself mysteriously, "it's just the man himself. Not his looks, not his background, not his potential—none of that—but the man himself."

Then, when Robert said, "Don't tell me you'd go to bed with that greaseball!", Margaret had had the nerve to arch her eyebrow, draw herself up stiffly, and announce: "I don't like you to speak that way to me, Robert. I won't have it!"

The very next afternoon, Robert had done a strange thing —most strange. He had gone shopping with Margaret this time; she had wanted his approval on a silk blouse. In the shop, once Margaret paid for the purchase, the change, in lire, was resting on the counter top. Before Margaret picked it up, Robert took some of the lire ($5 worth) and stuffed it into his own pocket. He simply stole it from her. Halfway down the street, Margaret counted her change and found the amount was too little. Robert let her go back to the store and complain unsuccessfully. In anger, Margaret refused the purchase she had just made at the store, though she had wanted the blouse very, very badly. She had punished the store for shortchanging her. Robert had let her go through all of that, simply by insisting he had payed no attention to the transaction. It was funny that it seemed to make up for the episode in the Fagianno; funny too, that one seemed to have something to do with the other, but that neither one was of any great importance. But there you were, it was another fragment from Robert Bowser's life—another nothing to add on to the nothings stretching across the years, and adding up now to this evening, to Raymond Battle.

In the middle of the English movie, which Raymond could concentrate on and was enjoying, the noise came again from the bedroom. Again he rushed in, turned on the light, and put the child on its back. This time the baby would not have any of it; she rolled over to her kneeling position and banged away.

Let her, Raymond thought. Let her bang the devil out of her little head—but he could not let her do that; each time her head hit, his own head ached in sympathy.

"Will you stop that?" he said to the child, who was fast asleep and bent on self-destruction with a will of iron. "Here, here!"

Each time he placed the child on its back, it charged back in the attack position. Ramond's heart began beating anxiously, and he felt a wave of acute anxiety begin in him. Was the child having a fit of some sort?

A voice from across the room, a squeaky, sleepy voice said, "Give her her stocking, Mister."

"Her what?" He turned and saw the four year-old sitting up, rubbing her eyes.

She said, "Chrissy won't head-bang if you give her one of Mommy's stockings to chew on."

"To chew on?"

"Umm hmmm. She goes to sleep with it, and she carries it around all day."

"Well, where is it?"

The child crawled out of bed before Raymond could stop her, and ran across to a bureau. She pulled open the bureau drawer, and out came a series of small leather books, each one announced by, "That's not it, that's not it, that's not it," as Raymond reached down and picked them up after her.

"Here it is!" she said. "Here's one of them." She pulled out a long silk stocking and ran across to the crib with it. "Here, Chrissy! Here's you 'tocking."

Raymond watched while the younger child reached up sleepily for the hose, took it in her little fist, put it to her mouth, and turned on her side, holding it as though it were a bottle.

"Now she'll sleep," said Carla Carson.

"Thank you," Raymond said.

Not until he was back in the living room did he discover he was carrying three leather-bound diaries.

He sat down and opened one.

The page was filled out in green ink.

NAME: BUNNY HILL CARSON (that's me!)
AGE: That would be telling!
WEIGHT: That would be too!
HEIGHT: 5'4"
COLOR OF HAIR: Bright red!
COLOR OF EYES: Baby-blue!
IN CASE OF ACCIDENT NOTIFY: THOMAS A.
    CARSON (hubby!)
    345 Alden Avenue
    St. Joseph, Missouri.
LIKES: Tommy Carson, Tom Carson, Thomas A.
    Carson.
DISLIKES: Sloppy kisses, wastebaskets that are full,
    liver!

At the bottom of the page, in a box made out in the same green ink used to answer the black printed queries above, were three notations.

1. April 3, 1953. First time I was ever asked to S.W.A.M. (NO!—of course!)
2. April 25, 1956. First time I ever S.W.A.M. (Okay, because it was Tommy A. Carson himself, my future hubby!)

3. June 15, 1957. I have now S.W.A.M. 156 times (T.A.C., natch, each time!)

Aloud, Raymond Battle exclaimed, "Good Lord!"

With a mixture of fascination, incredulity and revulsion, he turned to the next page.

THINGS I LIKE ABOUT HUBBY TOM

1. He is thoughtful and considerate. (Never goes in bathroom without asking me if I want to use it first.)
2. He is gentle.
3. He is especially kind when I am ill. (Hot water bottles and the whole bit!)
4. He has dreamy eyes.
5. He is very healthy and does not get sick like Al Crowler all the time!
6. He kisses better than anyone!
7. He is generous. (Example: The waffle iron he brought home when there was no occasion for it!)
8. He has a groovy body and uses it. The end!
9. He is very adaptable to circumstances. (Never once mentioned he could not stand singing tea-kettle until the night we had too many martinis at the Loxtons.)
10. He is mine, mine, mine, mine, my very own, my man!

Raymond Battle had a sudden impulse for a glass of wine. He got up and crossed to the decanter set out on the table with a half-dozen wine glasses.

"Hot water bottles and the whole bit," he murmured to himself as he poured the drink. "Good Lord!"

It was port, very sweet port. Not good port. He made a face after he swallowed it. He carried it back to the armchair, set it on the table, and reached across to turn down the sound on the television.

Then he began reading entries in the diary, at random.

He found that at the end of every month's record in the diary, there was a memoranda page. Invariably there was written across them: "Nothing at all" or "What do you expect?" or "Hate these pages. What's left to say?" Each diary entry ended with "Nite! Nite!" and began with, "Me again!"

This was Raymond Battle's sampling of Mrs. Carson's 1958 diary.

"Me again. Saw a movie tonight with Marlon Brando (slurp! slurp!) while Tommy worked late again. Nite! Nite!"

"Me again. I wish we could only wall-to-wall the living room. Nite! Nite!"

"Me again. Today I slept late and then cleaned fish bowl. Tomorrow is my birthday. Wonder what I'll get! Nite! Nite!"

"Me again. I do not like the cold. Ugh! Ugh! Tommy and I watched television until the end of Steve Allen. Wow, what a show! The guy is really hysterical! He had a swimming pool on stage tonight and was swimming in it, chasing ducks around it, etc. What a ball! Nite! Nite!"

"Me again. Today I finally did what Tommy wanted and went to the doctor's for the thing to protect me. The doctor was very nice about it and not at all embarrassed, which made it less embarrassing for me. He gave me a lovely blue and white zipper case to keep it in. Nite! Nite!"

"Me again. Today I got two pocketbook handles fixed at the shoemaker. Nite! Nite!"

On the very last page was the final entry.

"Me again. Incidentally, the change of ink from blue to red, since December 18, is because of all the Christmas cards I had to address. Christmas was really merry! It's such fun. I can't believe it's over! Well, bye bye 1958, you've been swell! Nite! Nite! Bye! Bye!"

Raymond Battle shut the diary and leaned back in the chair. Then, almost as though he were having a seizure of some sort, he leaned forward, shaking, holding himself around the waist—laughing, laughing in a crazy way he never had laughed before. Roaring!

When the door opened, he was still on his knees.

He looked up at her. "You're early," he said.

"Yes, I am. What are you doing?"

"I'm looking for something," he said. "I can't find it."

"Well, what is it?"

"It's nothing very much."

"Well, what?"

"It's just something that fell out of my eye," said Raymond Battle.

"Something that fell out of your eye!"

"Very well, Mrs. Carson, it's my left lens. A contact lens."

"Oh, do you wear those?"

"What would they be doing in my eyes, otherwise?"

"You don't have to be nasty, Mr. Battle."

"You weren't very nice to me earlier."

"I think you've been drinking, Mr. Battle. I know you have. There was a whole decanter of wine here, and it's empty."

"I'll replace it, if you like." Battle was crawling about by the television set, running the palms of his hands along the rug.

"I told you I didn't care if you had some. It's made you drunk, though."

Battle hit his forehead against the end of the low TV table. He cried out in pain, and held the injured part with his hand. He managed to say, "Sweet port is very sneaky, Mrs. Carson. One shouldn't have more than two small glasses of it."

"Do your lenses always fall out when you're drunk?" she asked. Battle could not see her very clearly without his other lens but he was aware she was standing near the mirror. Probably gawking at herself again, he thought, and he sighed and sat back on his haunches. "I can't find it! And the answer to your question, Mrs. Carson, is that I very, very seldom get drunk. In fact this is the first time, for your information."

"You can call me Bunny, Mr. Battle. Everyone does."

Battle heard the loud noise of her honking into her handkerchief. She said, "I have the most horrible hay fever. Worse at night." And more honking.

Battle got up on his feet. "Fortunately," he said, "the right lens fell into my lap."

"What made them fall out anyway?"

"I was laughing at something."

"I don't think I'd like wearing them very much at all, if
they fall out every time you laugh."

"I don't have that much to laugh about."

"That's too bad, Mr. Battle. Well, what are you going to
do about the lens?"

"Do you see it anywhere?"

She walked across the room and bent over at the spot on
the rug where Battle had been looking. "No . . . I might not
even know it if I did see it."

Battle squinted at her through his right eye, which contained a lens. She was wiping at her nose with a tissue
and staring down at the rug. Battle smelled something familiar, distasteful. He realized it was beer he smelled. He
said, "I'd say you were drinking too."

"Yes. There wasn't any rehearsal. The director just didn't
show. One of the boys did the funniest thing! There's this
blackboard in the room where we meet, and one of the
boys—his name is Scott Allen, and he's a riot—wrote on the
blackboard,

We was here when you was not,

Now you is here and we is not.

Just in case the director did show after all, natch!" She
straightened up and giggled. She repeated:

"We was here and you was not,

Now you is here and we is not!

Honestly, he's a riot! I had beer with him. He plays folk
songs on the guitar, real yummy."

"Well, I suppose there's not a thing I can do about it.
If you step on it, you step on it."

"What are you wearing contact lenses for, Mr. Battle?"

"There's nothing wrong with it, is there?"

"No, but it seems odd. You're not in theater or anything."

"No, I'm not in theater."

"Are you really writing a novel? Mrs. Plangman said
something about it."

"I'm making notes," said Battle. "Put it that way."

"Do you want some coffee? I might be a little tipsy myself. It doesn't take much."

"I could use a cup," said Battle.

"The girls okay?"

Battle followed her into the kitchen. He told her about
Chrissy banging her head, and about Carla giving the
stocking to her, and beyond that, he was unable to get a
word in. Mrs. Carson rattled on about Scott Allen, de-

scribing what he was majoring in at the University (drama, natch), what he was wearing that night (a yummy blazer with a yummy ascot), what he did last summer (a stock company in Skaneateles, New York; he was an understudy), and about his personality (real intellectual and cultured, but sweet at the same time).

Finally, Battle said, "You're certainly making a lot of him. How long have you known him, anyway?"

"I just met him tonight. He's trying out for the lead in the play, natch."

"Isn't he an undergraduate?"

"Umm hmm. A senior. You want sugar and cream, Mr. Battle?"

"Black," Battle said. "Isn't he a little young for you, Mrs. Carson?"

"He's twenty-three. I'm twenty-four. I was married very young, Mr. Battle. Very young!"

"How long have you been a widow, if I might ask?"

"A year last Tuesday."

"Your resiliency is admirable."

She whirled around and faced him, and he squinted back at her while she shouted, "Now, look! I don't need you coming up here making any cracks like that! I don't appreciate that at all, Mr. Battle!"

"Me coming up here! I was asked up here! I'm doing you a favor!"

"You just leave my resiliency out of it! I'm a young woman!"

"I never said you weren't."

"Just because you've had too many drinks!"

"Go ahead and marry your banjo player, for all I care, Mrs. Carson."

"He plays the guitar, goddam you!"

Battle backed away. "All right," he said, "The guitar—the banjo. Whatever it is he plays." Battle felt a peculiar delight in Mrs. Carson's anger. He felt immune to it—immune to her, as well. Preposterous person. He would drink his coffee and go back downstairs to his own place. He looked forward to taking off all his clothes and getting between the sheets, and he remembered he had changed the sheets that morning; they would be clean and cool. If only he had not lost one of his lenses, he would have no real regrets about his behavior this evening—none whatsoever. He had remembered to put back the diaries, and since reading them, he had absolutely no qualms about having drunk too much of the sweet port. He could be as tipsy as he liked around Mrs. Carson; it was just like being obstreperous and abnormal in some foreign country where you knew no one and no one knew you.

She handed him a coffee cup and he followed her back into the living room. He felt very much like announcing to her that sneakers did nothing for a woman's legs. Instead, he said, "And I'm not interested in those couple of dollars you put on top my stationery box when you came in, Mrs. Carson."

"It's payment for sitting."

"Ha! Ha! Payment for sitting! You knew I wouldn't take anything. You knew I'd offer my services, gratis. Now surely you knew that."

"What's biting you anyway, Mr. Battle? Why shouldn't you take it?"

"Even if I needed it, I wouldn't take it. Isn't it always the man who pays and pays. Ah yes! Waffle irons, hot water bottles and the whole bit! All lavished on you, hmmm?"

"You're so bombed you're out of your head." She giggled and blew her nose. "You are bombed!"

"Hot water bottles and the whole bit," he repeated, feeling it was slightly dangerous—but she missed the allusion altogether, and she only giggled harder.

Battle said, "True to you in my fashion, darling, except for a stray banjo player here and there."

He hit his mark. She was on her feet, shaking her finger at him, furious again. "Now, look! I don't know what your little game is all about, Mr. Battle, but don't bug me! You don't even know Scott, and you don't even know me! And I can just as easily pick up that telephone and tell Mrs. Plangman you're sitting up here insulting me!"

"Oh, that's typical. I'm sitting up here insulting you! What am I doing sitting up here?"

"Do you want a pound of flesh, Mr. Battle, because you babysat for a few hours?"

"Furthermore," said Battle, "it interests me that the baby has suicidal impulses."

"Head-banging is very common among babies, Mr. Battle. Goddam you! You're drunk! I'm a damn good mother, and you just shut up!"

"I wouldn't be at all surprised if Professor Bullard was

on his way up here right now," said Battle. "There's no point in screaming, Mrs. Carson."

"Just finish your coffee."

"I intend to."

"I think you're off your rocker, if you want to know."

"I don't care what you think, Mrs. Carson. Ha! Ha! You, least of all," said Battle, and again he began to laugh very loud, as he had earlier this evening, when he was by himself. He was amazed to see Mrs. Carson laughing too, laughing and blowing her nose, and murmuring, "Drunk as a skunk!" to herself. Then, he stopped laughing. A sharp needle of pain shot through his eyelid, and tears oozed out. His right lens was stuck up in the white of his eye, and in agony he made his way out of the room to the bathroom, where he flicked on the light button and grabbed a towel from the brass holder. He heard Mrs. Carson's footsteps following after him down the hall.

"Don't come in here!" he said. He knew he would be a spectacle, bending over the towel, while he pulled at his eyelid to force the object out. "I'll be all right."

"Are you getting sick?"

"My right lens!" he called. "It's my right lens!"

The pain was terrible, and he could hear her outside giggling. Then the lens popped out and into the towel. Raymond Battle took a step back, swayed, fell over with a great crash, and hit his head against the bathroom sink.

The next thing he knew, Mrs. Carson was kneeling beside him, wiping his forehead with a wet towel. He could not see her features at all clearly, but her voice was quite soft, and she was still giggling a bit, between words. "You're such a fool, Mr. Battle!" she was murmuring. "Just a ninny, really! You've cut your head, too. And now your right lens is lost."

"It's there in the towel," he muttered. "I caught it in the towel, just before I fell."

"Oh, no, Mr. Battle! I shook the towel out, to wet it."

Battle groaned. "God help me!" he said.

"Drunk as a skunk!" said Mrs. Carson, "Drunk as a skunk, you ninny!"

THIRTEEN

THE MORNING after, Raymond Battle woke up with a headache that did not allow him to remember everything right
away. The first thing he remembered, as he turned over in
his bed, and clutched himself around the waist to comfort
his aches, was the diary. Pffft! Pssss! He made several little
deprecating noises, pleased that he was able to think of
something to make himself feel superior on this most in-
ferior day. Then for a very few seconds he struggled with
the code he had been unable to decipher the night before—
s.w.a.m. He thought of s.w.a.k. (sealed with a kiss, a code
from his younger days), then the possibilities of s: sex, sin,
...some other s words, and onto w...and finally, he
broke the code. Sleep with a man! Of course! Oh, Lord...
Lordgod...deprecating noises...and he rolled over.

Then it came back, the inevitable playback, right through
to her helping him up from the bathroom floor, out of the
apartment and down to this very room.

"Can you get out of your clothes all right?" she had asked.

Oh, Lord...Lordgod...and thank God, she had gone
back up and left him, almost immediately!

Suddenly (and because Robert Bowser had never once
been drunk; high, but not without his senses), Raymond
Battle understood the dismal facial expressions of John Hark
on the morning after. He read Hark with a new language, the
language of empthy and same-boatism.

He was afraid to get out of bed and apply this language
to his own reflection in the mirror; afraid, and physically
incapable of doing it. He was a prisoner of the bed and
thoughts-in-bed-when-one-is-too-hungover to rise from bed.
Hell, was all; it was hell.

He decided to have nothing more to do with the occupants
of apartment 3. Not that he had ever had anything to do
with them really. But now he would hire a man to take care
of the upper floors. That part of his routine was over. He
would keep entirely to himself, even though he knew he was
going to have to fight off his loneliness. He would spend his

time planning ahead. So far there was very little he could do but plan, since he was still too new to the police's Wanted sheet and since Plangman would certainly help the police to find him. But it would take a lot of planning anyway; a lot of very careful planning. He wanted to buy a book on Canada; more and more, Canada seemed the place. He wanted to get someplace far away; he wanted, perhaps more than he wanted anything else, to get out now from under Plangman's thumb. He would have to admit to himself that Plangman's plan was a working one, that it was a safe hiding place—probably the safest Bowser could ever hope for. Still, Bowser was beginning to hate the fact that, in a sense, he was the victim of the type of person he had always been repelled by, afraid of—which one was it? Perhaps it was fear—it was knowing how close he was, pushed a little this way and a little that, to being the same sort of fool— simply a more substantial sort. But it was not just the feeling of being Plangman's victim now; it was the almost certain knowledge that in the future, Plangman would victimize him much, much more. He knew Harvey thought he had a great deal of money; Harvey, he knew, would be back for it. Yes, he had to escape Plangman. He had been a Lotus-eater long enough, far too long. He decided that right this very moment, he was in grave danger—danger that was moving in very slowly, like some lazy but inevitable fog— coming at him. The newspapers had not played up the thing very big at all—a mention or two after the initial announcement of the embezzlement—a photograph—not very much more. Things, on the surface, seemed to go along too smoothly. Plangman was bringing off his end of the bargain with suspicious placidity. Something was in the wind; Bowser just had that feeling.

He would not write Bud Wilde. He trusted Bud, but by this time it seemed not unlikely that Wilde's mail might be watched. Whatever he planned, he would have to accomplish on his own. In a moment of extreme weakness, he played with the idea of sneaking back to New Hope, of walking in his back door and simply confronting Margaret and asking for her help.

He groaned. No, no, no! On his own. On his own.

He turned over on his side again and thought of Mrs. Carson and her banjo player. Probably, within a year, Margaret would have run off with someone or moved someone in. La donne mobile ... Well, let her! Let them both run around, for that matter. He decided that he hated Mrs. Carson. She was a cheap, little, redheaded slut. He wished he had told her so last night, since he would not be speaking to her again. He wished he had added that he had never in his life before encountered such an insipid, meaningless, boring, stupid person, with her diaries and her me again——nite nites!

Lordgod, he was so very far away from anything he knew. He shut his eyes. He could see a desk, a report—his own words on it, his own pure, mathematical, quick, clean logic: "... and the board of directors should reduce the quarterly dividened because of disappointing operations in the fiscal year ended——"

"Yes," he said aloud. He murmured to himself: "The company will pay a dividend of 25 cents a share to stockholders on record of ... No, no, no ... on my own now."

His "on his own" voice echoed in his memory:

"Go ahead and marry your banjo player, for all I care, Mrs. Carson."

Raymond Battle decided that the first thing he would do, would be to go into St. Louis for new lenses. He had an insurance policy just in case something like this happened. He would take a bus and get new ones; there would be no reason in the world why he would ever have to be confronted by Mrs. Carson again. If she were to knock on his door to say she had found the lenses, he would simply not answer her. Cut her off cold, out!

As soon as he was able, he dressed and put on his rimless glasses, and arrived in St. Louis shortly before four that afternoon.

He returned very late that evening, too late even for the late show on television. Before he went to bed, he wrote an angry letter about his extreme poverty to Plangman, destroyed it, and then studied a map of the United States. He fell asleep looking at it, dreamed of meeting Bud Wilde in Mexico (Bud told him that he had paid back all the money Robert had embezzled; Robert was free!), and woke up in the morning feeling better.

He was in the kitchen, timing his tea to be done by the time his toast was buttered, when he heard the pounding at his door.

"Hallo?" he called. "Who is it?"

"You let me in!" was the answer, the command, really—— and a very angry one. Mrs. Carson.

"I'm having my breakfast, Mrs. Carson," said he. "I'm hiring a man to do the work around here. I'm not available any more."

"You goddam well make yourself available, or I'll kick in your door!"

"What?" Raymond Battle said it to himself in a whisper. His face was pinched up with utter confusion. He walked very gingerly to the door and opened it a crack. The next thing he knew, the door was slammed into his jaw, slammed shut —and there she was.

"Look here, young lady," he began. He was stunned into silence by a swift, hard punch on his nose.

"You listen to me, you creep!" said she, "Don't sit up in my place writing letters about me to people! The next time you write one of your stupid letters about me to people, don't leave it around in my wastebasket!"

"That's a nice habit," said Raymond Battle, "reading other people's mail."

"It's my habit to empty my wastebasket! And I don't need letters in it about how vacant I am, or about my hay fever! I could write a few hundred letters about you too, you know, Mr. Battle! About your silly lenses and your wine drinking, and that goddam baseball cap you wear around! You're so superior, are you? You old creep!"

"Is that all you have to say to me?" said Battle. "Because I'm about to eat my breakfast!"

"You can shove your breakfast!"

"You certainly are a nice young lady, Mrs. Carson."

"You can take this and shove it too!" she said. She threw the wadded-up piece of stationery at Battle, kicked his ankle, and slammed out the door. The door sprang open again with the force.

"Little bitch!" Battle said, hopping on one foot, holding his ankle. "Dirty little bitch!"

He hobbled over to close the door and heard her shouting from the third floor: "And after I was nice to you the other night! Well, you'll get yours, Mr. Battle!"

FOURTEEN

HARVEY PLANGMAN rushed about making last minute improvements in an already elegant scene. He was serving highballs in his new scorecard glasses, for which he had sent away. Each one bore the crest of a luxurious country club. He saved the one from the Seminole Club, in Palm Beach, for Hayden Cutler. That was the most impressive of the lot; anything connected with Palm Beach impressed Plangman.

On his desk, under the initial-P paperweight, with the rich Florentine-gold finish, he had placed four or five travel folders from B.O.A.C., Panagra, Air France, and the Cunard Line This was to tip off the Cutlers that Harvey was interested in a trip abroad, just as they were. Yesterday, Harvey had gone over his finances and figured out that he had $3700 left of the ten, including ownership of his new MG. If it were necessary, he could sell the MG. If things moved as slowly as they were, it was possible he would have to finance his own European trip in order to go along with the Cutlers. But first things were first; first, he must be invited to join them. When either one noticed the folders (he had placed them smack in the middle of his desk; who could ignore them?) he would simply say, "Yes, I've been thinking of taking a leave of absence from school. I feel the need of travel. Broadens the horizons, y'know."

In his kitchen, at the leather-covered bar from which he served drinks, Harvey had the liquor bottles lined up, with their labels showing. He was particularly proud of his bottle of Zubrovka vodka.

"It's a very interesting vodka," he planned to say, "flavored with buffalo grass, you know." He had read that in the advertisement for Zubrovka, and sure enough, the bottle itself contained a single blade of grass. Then there was a bottle of Old Smuggler, naturally, and Dry Sack, Beefeater gin, Old Bushmills Irish whisky, and Grand Marnier liqueur. The bottles had been delivered from the liquor store only that afternoon. Harvey had opened each one and poured

118

out a little, to give the impression they were everyday
items around his place, and not special for the Cutlers.

In the hall mirror, he checked his appearance. He was
wearing his new Burberry jacket, his Sulka shirt, and a dark
blue Countess Mara tie (the crown and C.M. showed better
against a dark background, he had learned). Since Boy
Ames had complained that Pour Un Homme smelled like
perfume, he had switched to St. John's Bay Rum after-
shave, which he had splashed on his face and the backs of
his hands after showering. His hair style was changed too,
from the longish, high-swept look to a very severe short-
cropped style. The latter had been Bowser's suggestion, one
of his few. For all Bowser had helped, Plangman might
still be very much the same person. But he had not stood
still, or stopped at Bowser's few crumbs. He had most
definitely taken things into his own hands.

At the sound of his downstairs bell, his heart thudded. He
hummed a little snatch of "Some Enchanted Evening", and
glided across to press the release on the front door.

"Now, I've taken you at your word," he planned to say.
"I haven't fussed with dinner. It's a very simple Roman
meal. Everyday fare, in Rome."

He chuckled to himself while he waited for the elevator
to deliver them. "When in Plangman's," he said aloud, "do
as the Romans do." La, la, de, da, la—he felt tip-top tonight; tip-top!

To his surprise, Lois Cutler was alone.

"Where's your father?" he said.

"Aren't you going to ask me in?"

He stepped back and held open the door. "Is he joining
you here?"

She swept past him, handing him her coat. She said,
"Daddy's not coming. He has some business. He'll pick me
up later. I told him to just beep the bell twice, as a signal."

"Beep the bell twice! You mean, he's not even coming
up?"

"Mais non, Monsieur. Pas de tout."

"Well, that's a fine thing. I was expecting him for dinner."

"You can freeze his portion, Monsier, or have it for
lunch tomorrow. Old love-head can't make it."

"I certainly didn't expect this," said Harvey.

"Dumkins is not exactly predictable."

She settled herself on the couch, while Harvey hung up

her coat, noticing the label as he put it on the hanger.
Bloomingdale's? He was surprised, let down. The whole
evening was starting off badly. He walked into the living-
room and said, "Come into the kitchen while I make us a
drink."

"Oh, cheri, I'm too bushed! Make it for me, hmm, and
bring it in?"

Harvey sighed. "Very well."

"Well, is it such an effort?"

"Nein, nein, Frau Cutler," said Harvey. "I just wanted
company. But nein, never mind . . . Would you like some
vodka? I have some very interesting vodka with buffalo . . ."

"Scotch," said Lois. "On the rocks, s'il vous plait."

"Buffalo grass," Harvey finished. "Then you want Old
Smuggler?"

"Please, on the rocks."

"Ganz bestimmt?" said Harvey smiling.

"What?"

"It's German. I said, are you sure? This vodka . . . wait,
let me show you the   bottle . . ."

But she waved the idea away with her hand and said,
"No, no, no, I really don't want vodka."

Harvey fixed her a Scotch and took it into her. Then
he put ice and tonic in the scorecard glass from the Seminole Club, and carried the glass and the bottle of Zubrovka
into the living room. He set them on the marble-top coffee table, and turned to Lois, who was standing by his
desk.

"Ah," he said, "noticing my travel folders, hmm?"

She wandered back to the couch and sat down. "Are
you going away?"

"Yes, yes, I might. Travel is broadening, as the cliché
puts it."

"Where are you going?"

"Oh, I haven't anything definite in mind." He glanced down
at the desk and saw the top folder, the one from the Medi-
terranean Black Sea Cruise Corporation. He took in five or
six names fast, picked up his glass from the coffee table,
and said, "Perhaps to Las Palmas, Casablanca, Malta, Alex-
andria, Haifa—I don't know. The Greek islands, perhaps.
Rhodes . . . the Greek islands."

Lois Cutler said, "Daddy says none of the Greek islands,
none of them, can hold a candle to Nantucket. Daddy

says, if you want to go to an island, why go halfway
across the world when there's Nantucket, where at least the
food is edible. Daddy likes cities. Rome, Paris, Florence."

"My little dinner this evening is a Roman dish," said
Harvey.

"Daddy and I will probably go to Europe in November.
Have you ever heard of Adair Trowbridge?"

"No, who's she?" Harvey held up the bottle of Zubrovka
and poured the vodka into his glass. He pointed to the
blade of grass and murmured, "Buffalo grass," smiling at
Lois.

"It's not a she, it's a he," said Lois, ignoring the blade
of grass in the bottle. "Adair Trowbridge. He's a horticultural photographer. He's the one who wrote me from Europe, in French."

"Well, I've never heard of him. As a matter of fact, I
like cities better myself. I was telling this buddy of mine—
name of Boy Ames . . . he's on the Mercantile Exchange . . .
I was telling him the other night at the Plaza, that I have
a yen to see Paris, Rome, Belgium, Florence. I like cities
better myself."

"Was this the other night that you called?"

"Yes. I explained that the next day, didn't I? I guess we
had a little too much to imbibe. I hope your father wasn't
—angry."

"He said you said he was beautiful."

Harvey felt his face flame. "I said he was a beautiful
person. I certainly never said he was beautiful! Do you
think I'd call a man up and tell him he was beautiful?
That's very unfair of your father, Lois!"

"Dumkins was only teasing. You know old love-head!"
She laughed and traced the sweat bubbles on her highball
glass, as though she were running her fingers along Hayden
Cutler's cherished brow. "He's just a big dumb," she said in
a dreamy voice.

"As a matter of fact," Harvey said, "I don't know 'old
love-head.' " It seems to me he doesn't give me a chance
to know him. I've done everything too. What about that
birthday party I gave him?"

"He was very appreciative, Harvey."

"Well, he could have come to dinner, it seems to me."

"He just couldn't," Lois answered. There seemed to be
no retort for that one. Harvey let it go. He said, "Shall
I put on the hi-fi?"

"I'm hungry, Harvey."

"But we haven't finished one drink."

"Daddy's picking me up at ten, and it's eight-thirty now. I don't want to keep him waiting."

"At ten? Ten o'clock? That's a fine thing. I mean, that gives us very little time, Lois."

"I didn't even have any lunch. We were over at Adair's studio."

"It's a silly name for a man to have," Harvey said.

"I like it. Can't we eat soon, Harvey?"

He had set a very smart table in the small dining alcove off the living room. He had bought a long fringe-edged table cloth, tangerine colored, with ruby-red napkins to accompany it. The young man in the store on Madison Avenue, where he made the purchases, said it was a daring color scheme, and with white plates, the table would be "simply smart." He had bought a long wine basket, to cradle the bottle of Bordeaux, and he had memorized a little something he had read on a wine chart, which he would recite when he opened the wine. He did not feel very much at all like tangerine table cloths, ruby-red napkins, or memorized conversational bits any more; he worked in the kitchen at getting the dinner on, peeved and hurt at Hayden Cutler. At last he had managed to get Lois to call her father at his club, to ask him if he wouldn't stop in when he came to pick her up. He could hear her in there talking with him.

". . . not yet," she was saying. "Oh, I will . . . Ummm, hmmm. Yes, dumkins . . . then you don't think it's a good idea?"

Harvey slammed the frying pan around on the stove at her last words, then hushed himself to hear still more.

"God bless me," she was saying, "and God bless you. Keep each one and keep us two."

Then she made that smacking noise with her lips. "Here's a kiss!" she said, "Bye, bye."

Harvey called in, "Then he's not coming?"

"Nope. 'Fraid not, Monsieur."

"Dinner's served," Harvey said sourly.

"Sursum corda?" said Lois Cutler.

But he pulled himself together somewhere between the kitchen and the dining alcove. He even managed a smile. The way to Hayden Cutler's heart could not be reached via his stomach this evening, but it could be reached via his daughter any evening. Harvey had to remember that. Still, he was slightly on edge. He had never realized before that he was not doing at all well, really. Badly, in fact. Again he remembered his bank balance. It had gone down very, very fast.

He picked up the bottle of Bordeaux by the neck, and smiled at Lois across the candlelight. "Burgundy is good with this dish," said he, "but they had only 1955 Burgundy at my local place, and I'm afraid nature was not very kind in the gently sloping hills of Burgundy during the 1955 harvest."

Lois said, "You should order from Sherry's. They have all years."

"So I got Bordeaux," Harvey ended his speech feebly.

Then Lois Cutler looked down at her plate and said, "Is this raw egg?"

"Spaghetti alla carbonara," Harvey said grandly. "A Roman dish."

"Well, maybe the Romans can stand raw egg yolks, but ugh and ugh! I can't."

"Just mix it in. You won't even know it. There's sage in there. The sage offers a little extra touch that . . ."

"Won't even know it! I'll know it! I can see it! Ugh, Harvey, mon Dieu! I can't eat raw egg yolk."

"What do you want me to do?"

"Just get it out of my sight. Please! Honestly, Harvey, I think it'll make me sick."

"I'll take the egg yolk off," Harvey said, getting up and removing the plate from in front of her. "I'll take it in the kitchen and remove the egg yolk."

"It'll still have egg slime on it. No, I'm sorry. The Romans may think it's both divine and dav-oon, but pour moi, ugh! Oh, God, it's just a good thing dumkins didn't come! If there's even the slightest leakage in his breakfast eggs, he always says, 'Take it back, I can still see the chicken!' "

"That must improve everybody's appetite," said Harvey.

"Well, that's the way dumkins and I feel about eggs."

"What'll I do?" Harvey said, standing there with the plate. "Let me just take off the egg. There won't be any slime on it. I'll mix it all in for you."

"No, really. Just take it away. Anyway, I think I've lost my appetite. I'll have a roll and some butter."

Harvey took the plate into the kitchen. He opened the refrigerator, but there was nothing in it to offer her. He opened the kitchen cabinet, and there was nothing there either, not even a can of soup. He walked back into the alcove. Lois was buttering a roll. There was a lit cigarette on the ashtray beside her.

"I'll just have some bread and wine," she said.

"I can't sit here and eat without you."

"Go ahead, Monsieur. It's my own fault if I don't like raw egg yolk."

Harvey sat down. "In Rome, it's an everyday dish," he said. "I think you're going to be very disappointed when you go to Europe."

"I'll struggle along on lombatine di vitello at Alfredo's," she said. "I've been to Rome three times and I've never had raw egg yolk."

"What's lombatine di vitello?"

"Grilled veal chops. Very good."

"Well, if you want to be a tourist."

"Since love-head and I are New Hopeians and pas Romans, cheri, it seems a bit inevitable that we'll be tourists, n'est-ce pas?"

"I mean, behave like tourists."

"Ugh!" she said, "I can't even watch you eat it."

"It's all mixed in now. You can't even see the egg."

"And I was even going to kiss you goodbye tonight," Lois said. She picked up her cigarette and blew a cloud of smoke, sipped the wine and said, "Anyway, the wine's trés bon."

"What do you mean you were even going to kiss me good night. We always kiss good night."

"I said 'goodbye'."

"But you're not going away until November. Besides," Harvey smiled shyly and slyly, "I might see you over there."

Lois got up from the table and walked into the other room. "I'll be back directly," said she. "Sit tight, Monsieur."

She came back with her pocketbook. From it, she took a folded clipping cut from a newspaper. "Did you see last Sunday's *Tribune*?"

"No."

"I'll wait until you've finished."

"What have you got there? Show me now."

"No, finish up, first."

Harvey pushed his plate away. "I don't enjoy the dish very much—not any more," he said, in a poutish voice. It made no dent on Lois, who said, "I don't wonder."

"What do you have there?"

"It's a clipping from last Sunday's *Tribune*. Voila!" She handed it to him.

GARDEN WITHOUT A SINGLE FLOWER was the heading. Plangman looked at the picture to the side of the article. It showed a man seated sideways at a small round table, which contained a bottle of wine and one table setting. The man was holding a long cigarette holder. He was wearing a scarf of some sort knotted about his neck, a boatneck sweater, slacks, and sandals. Under the picture, the caption read:

"Adair Trowbridge at lunch in his studio garden. Ferns, ivy, crab-apple, willow, and privet are planted by a sapling fence. Feather rocks and wooden ducks add to the setting. A four-tier fountain decorates the east side."

The article began, "Mr. Trowbridge, a horticultural photographer, is an authority on ferns and other plants. At his studio in New Hope, Pennsylvania, his garden does not contain a single flower...."

Two long columns discussed his flowering crab ensemble, his Spanish wrought-iron gates, his privet hedge divider, and his Hankow screw willows.

The article concluded: "Mr. Trowbridge has his lunch on the terrace each day and it is always the same—raw vegetables of several kinds with tuna fish and a pint of white wine, no bread, butter or anything else."

Plangman handed back the clipping. "Well?" he said, "What about it?"

"That's Adair."

"What has he to do with me?"

Lois Cutler smiled. "He has to do with moi, cheri. You see, Adair and I have been writing back and forth in French, while he was in Europe—you knew that, oui? That I was writing this man in French? Well, viola. I guess we just . . . we're going to be engaged. He's home now, and we decided it very suddenly."

Harvey Plangman stared at her.

"That's the reason Daddy felt it was better that he didn't come tonight," she said. "I told him I was going to tell you about Adair and me."

FIFTEEN

At the top of the stairs that morning, little Chrissy Carson was sitting with her mother's stocking in her mouth, singing to herself:

"Peck up all your cars and woe,
He I go, singing low,
Bye, bye, black-burd ———"

She called out to Raymond Battle, who was on his way to his mailbox, on the front porch. "Ga-mornin' Misser Bat-ul!"

"Hullo!" Battle said. "Don't fall down the stairs!" he added gruffly.

"Done faw down 'tairs!" she called back.

On Saturday, in his mailbox, Battle had found an envelope containing his left lens. Inside was a note:

Dear Mr. Battle,
This must be one of your eyes. I haven't come across the other one yet. I think you are the rudest man I ever met!

Sincerely, Vacant Bunny Carson.

He had seen her (without her seeing him; he had peeked through his doorway at her) three or four times over the weekend. He knew her footsteps on the stairs very well—the rhythm was constant, a rush down three, a bounce where she skipped one, a rush down three more, another bounce—a crash at the bottom. He discovered that she had a whole wardrobe of those Ked sneakers, a pair to match every outfit. His glimpse of her was usually of her legs. He would see the hem of the skirt, the white freckled skin, then the bright blue Ked trademark on the white rubber, and the shoe matching the skirt's color. Her legs looked like bowling pins turned upside down.

Once, she had come down the stairs with a man, and Raymond had guessed it was Scott Allen. From time to time

127

during the long weekend, he had heard Allen up there singing. There was one song he heard over and over:

> By and by,
> By and by,
> Stars shining brightly in the sky, by and by,
> O Lord!

He would hear the sounds of Allen strumming the guitar,
the sounds of all of them singing—Allen, the children, Mrs.
Carson and Mrs. Hill. There was always a great deal of
laughter and clapping of hands, and a few times Raymond
Battle had to use all his self-control to keep from calling
on the phone to complain of the noise. Sunday morning
Battle had dreamed of Mrs. Carson. In the dream she was
standing in a doorway on a New York City street. There was
a familiar expression on her countenance. He had said, "You
were in some other dream. What are you doing back?"
That was all; he had awakened. He remembered when he
woke up that he had seen that expression once long ago, on the
face of an actual woman in a doorway in New York City. Or
was it a man? It was something to do with two people looking
at one another, one of them with love spelled out in all his
features in such a strange, real way, that at the time Robert
Bowser had felt as though something were being taken away
from him—an emptiness.

> By and by,
> By and by,
> Stars shining brightly in the sky, by and by,
> O Lord!

He could not get the song out of his head; he went about
humming it, and alternately telling himself it was his duty
to inform Mrs. Plangman that Mrs. Carson was seeing men
in her apartment. The trouble was there was no rule against
it. Mrs. Carson did not come under University control, since
she was only an auditor in most courses, and not under
age or under the control of anyone. Her mother was living
with her, and Battle was certain Allen was not spending
the night there. It amounted to nothing.

Raymond had gotten one good look at Allen. He was an
unkempt fellow who looked as though he never washed, and
wore colored shirts unbuttoned halfway down his chest, and

large belts with great brass buckles. His hair was too long; his pants were too tight; his eyes, too cock-sure. He was a fellow who would amount to nothing, Raymond Battle decided; a fellow, who in all probability, was at the high point of his life right now—what had come before and what would come after, was all downhill. "Banjo" Raymond called him, to himself: he would think: "...so she has Banjo up there again!"

On the porch, in his mailbox, there was nothing for Battle but a bill from the eye doctor in St. Louis. Nothing from Plangman, which was unusual for a Monday. He saw a car pull up in front of 702, the back seat filled with children. The car parked at the curb, the motor running, and then from the house came Mrs. Carson with Chrissy and Carla.

He stepped aside.

"Done faw down 'tairs!" Chrissy said to him. She was still carrying the stocking, holding on to her mother's hand.

Carla said, "You're the man that sat with us. You're Mr. Battle."

Mrs. Carson went by him without a word.

Battle walked back in the house. When he was almost to his door, he heard the front door open and close, heard Mrs. Carson say, "I still haven't located your other eye, Mr. Battle."

The children were not with her now.

He said, "They're not glass eyes, you know. They're contact lenses. I have another pair, thank you."

"You look much better without your baseball cap."

He was not prepared for a nice word. He grunted something—made some sort of noise, and stood there. Then he said, "Where are the children? Out playing in the street?"

"Oh, you're so sweet, Mr. Battle! Doesn't everyone tell you what a sweet man you are?"

"Never mind. Your problem," Battle mumbled, turning to go into his apartment.

"The children," she said, "have joined a nursery. They were just picked up, or couldn't you see that far?"

She was wearing a cotton house dress—violet-colored, with violet-colored Keds. She seemed very short to Battle, who was extremely tall. He looked down at her, and she met his glance with clear, unsmiling eyes. She said, "Do you want to call a truce?"

"I'm not at war with you, Mrs. Carson."

"Would you like to come up for coffee?"

It was Margaret who used to say it: that she could always guess the age of an author by the love scenes in his novel. In a young author's novel they were always very long and suspenseful and tempest-tossed, described almost dutifully, as though the author had been to some country where no one else had been, and must capture its climate for the reader. "Like all travelogues," Margaret used to say, "they please the narrator the most. And the author less young, middle-aged, was very likely to simply put it down in three words: They became lovers. Margaret used to laugh and say, "It sounds more obscene than all the youthful elaboration somehow, the same way coitus always sounded to me like a four-letter word."

Raymond Battle remembered Margaret's saying that over and over, in the week following the invitation for coffee from Mrs. Carson. She was Bunny now. He was used to sitting on the bed up in 3, watching her peel off her clothes and kick off her Keds prior to pushing him back on the mattress (always smiling; it irritated him); used to the daylight of the room which in the beginning inhibited him, so that he used to stay in his shorts, and accustomed, as well, to her periodic, triumphant reminders that he must not think she was vacant any longer. They had become lovers, just like in the older author's novel, with very little fanfare and even less suspense. It was a little like morning gymnastics, Raymond Battle decided, and he didn't wonder; hadn't he read her diaries? When she fell on top of him; at approximately ten-forty-five every morning, he had the annoying memory of her "Me Again" and afterwards, "Nite! Nite!" The fact was, it was obscene. She had a body that ripped right through him when he saw it uncovered; she was one of those women who look fabulous naked, and not nearly so voluptuous clothed. She was also little interested in receiving any gratification herself, another factor that lent an air of obscenity to the proceedings; and then too, she talked about it too much. It was Raymond Battle's own fault for asking questions, he supposed. Still, he wished she would have the good sense to put him off. Margaret had had such sense. He had only that much to go by for comparison. But after, when they would lie in bed and talk, it seemed to Raymond what little feeling there had been, went with their words.

"You don't seem to really enjoy it," he would say.

"I like it if you do, though."

"But, don't you see, I'd like it better if you would."

"It takes me too long. I have to think of things."

"What do you mean?"

"You'll laugh."

"I certainly won't. After all, nothing's strange that accomplishes satisfaction. Don't be so conventional."

He was actually very much in the dark about what she had to think about; what was there to think about? He remembered the night in Paris, when Margaret had been unable to concentrate because of the street noises. He was not at all certain he wanted the puzzle solved.

"All right," said Bunny Carson, "I have to picture something in my mind."

He decided not to encourage her. She went on anyway. "You know," she said. "Something from a book I've read or something like that."

"What book?"

"Oh, it doesn't have to be a particular book. Some best seller."

"Some dirty part or something?"

"You said it, I didn't. If you want to call it—dirty."

"All right, sexy," said Raymond. Well, there you have it, he thought. He felt depressed.

"Yes, sexy," she said.

A refrain from some old song came to Raymond's mind: ". . . well, if this isn't love, it'll have to do . . . until the real thing comes along."

For a week then, it went that way. Mrs. Hill had taken a job in a jewelry store, and the children were off at the nursery school. They were lovers, without any words of love exchanged, without any modesty, and with no restraint. Raymond Battle found that he was extremely inventive and imaginative; Robert Bowser was slightly shocked, often looking down his nose at the whole sordid mess. One morning in the middle of the week, as Battle was getting into his pants, he said, "You know, Bunny, I read your diaries."

He expected her to blow up. That was gone too.

She answered. "There's nothing in my diaries."

"Exactly," he answered.

"You're not going to get me to fight with you again, Ray," she answered. "That's all in the past."

"Oh?"

"I don't care what you think. If you really thought I was so terrible, you wouldn't be coming up here every morning."

"Haven't you ever heard of a man seeing a woman for just one reason?"

She said, "I've never heard of a man telling a woman he was seeing her for just one reason. Why should he tell her? You just want to get me to react. Well, I won't."

"Don't."

"Don't worry, I won't!"

"I won't come up here any more either."

"Have it your way, Ray." She went on applying Quik-Polish to her Keds. She was sitting on the side of the bed without any clothes on.

Raymond Battle said, "Vacant is an understatement."

He went downstairs that day thoroughly disgusted with her. Well, it was over, and he was glad. He spent the afternoon washing his clothes and cleaning the apartment. He went to the early movie at the Uptown, and afterward, had a soda in a shop where the Stephens College girls hung out. Most of them were only three or four years younger than she was; he studied them. They reminded him of Margaret at that age. There was something about them. Class, Plangman would have called it. Plangman was right. On his way out of the shop he bought a china rabbit with lollipops stuck in its tail, and the next morning he took it up to Bunny to give to Chrissy.

·"Is that all?" she said in the doorway.

"Ask me in," he said quietly, solemnly.

She said, "The door's open. You can walk in, but I won't ask you in."

He was back in it again.

It was at the week's end, on late Saturday night. Mrs. Hill had taken the children to St. Louis, and it was their first evening together. Raymond had cooked spaghetti alla carbonara for their dinner, and he had bought a bottle of red wine.

They lingered over the wine and cigarettes at the end of the meal, and she was tight.

"I never knew you could cook so good!" she was saying.

"There wasn't anything to it."

"So fancy! With the raw egg on top. I never had anything like it before, Ray."

"I'm glad you liked it."

"It was yummy! You're sweet."

It was the first endearment she had ever offered, and it

pleased Battle. He actually leaned across the table and kissed
her. She clung to him with a sudden force murmuring,
"Red wine and everything; it was so nice and yummy!"

It was the first time, too, that they had been unable to
wait out the walk down the hall to the bedroom. They made
love in the living room, on the floor. It was her first time too.

"What book was it?" Raymond Battle smiled afterward.

"No book."

"Honestly?"

"I swear it!" she said. "It's never happened before."

"I guess the answer is a bottle of red wine."

"Natch!" she giggled. "Or raw egg yolk."

They laughed and Raymond Battle felt good. When the
phone rang, he said, "Let it ring."

"I can't. It's probably Mother."

"Does she know anything?"

"She thinks you're very mysterious," Bunny said, getting
up to answer the phone. "She says you don't look or act
like what you are."

"What am I?" He put the pillow over him, sat up and lit
a cigarette.

"Sweet," she said, disappearing into the other room.

He leaned against the couch, smoking the cigarette. He had
a really good feeling. He felt the way Bowser used to wonder
what it was like to feel, a way Margaret would have said was
not like him at all. It wasn't either. He shut his eyes and
smiled. He thought of how it had been making love with
Bunny a moment ago—and then he remembered the poem
Bud Wilde had tacked up in their room at Princeton:

> "Why do you walk through the fields in gloves,
>   When the grass is as soft as the breast of doves.
>   And shivering-sweet to the touch."

He remembered what Plangman had said months ago, back
at the Black Bass, about there being a reason why their lives
had been completely changed by each other. "I believe there's
a reason it was you, in particular, and me, in particular,"
Plangman had said.

"Hey, hurry back!" Raymond Battle called out. He felt
very high himself, but not on wine. He grinned and hugged
the pillow to him, and thought how good it was to be the
first one with a woman—not her first man, but the first time.

"No book about it!" he said aloud, laughing.

She walked in as he said it. He was glad she hadn't put anything on.

"What did you say?"

"I said, no book."

She smiled. "That's right, Ray. Even with Tommy I never . . ."

"Don't talk it all away now," he said, reaching for her. She came down and curled into him, and he kissed her for a long time. He looked at her a minute. "Don't smile," he said.

"All right."

"I love you, Bunny," he said. He was testing again—testing the sound of those words—they were okay, and he meant it. For a fraction of a second after he said them, he thought he would hear the familiar response. "Why do you suddenly announce it? You must know what prompted it. Go back over it. I was saying that I hadn't seen round butter balls in . . ."

Bunny's eyes searched his solemnly. "Thank you," she answered.

"I love you, Bunny," he said again.

"But now you're smiling, after you told me not to."

"It's all right," he said holding her. "It's okay."

She said, "Except we have to get dressed, Ray."

"Why should we? Let's make love again."

"That was Scott on the phone."

"Banjo? What'd he want?"

"He's coming over. He's bringing his guitar."

"Tonight? At quarter to twelve?"

"He just got out of rehearsal, Ray. He says he wants to make me feel better, because I didn't get the part in the play."

Raymond Battle simply stared at her.

She said, "Oh, you're included, Ray! If you want to be. You'll like him. Did I ever tell you what he wrote on the blackboard that time the director didn't show up? He wrote, 'We was here when you was not . . .' "

"Now you is here and we is not," Raymond Battle finished it.

"Don't tell me you're angry," she said, "after the nice time we had."

SIXTEEN

THE MOMENT Harvey Plangman saw Adair Trowbridge, he felt reassured. Trowbridge and the Cutlers had been watching home movies of some sort when Harvey rang the bell. Trowbridge was standing by the projector in the living room, while Lois and her father hung back near the entranceway, speaking to one another in very low voices. Harvey knew they were talking about him. He had not chanced a phone call to announce his arrival. His phone conversations the past week with Lois were most unsatisfactory. The best thing to do, he had decided, was to make a personal appearance. He was glad Trowbridge was there at the time. He had wanted that; he had prepared for it. He had read up on ferns, enough to carry on a small conversation about them— shoe-string ferns, rattlesnake ferns, interrupted ferns, and young fern leaves, or fiddleheads. Why shouldn't he and Trowbridge be friends, after all?

His feeling of reassurance stemmed from the fact Trowbridge was very short, and rather plump. Certainly not what Harvey had expected. Instantly, Harvey felt rather patronizing toward Trowbridge. He extended a warm hand and grinned at the fellow. "Hello, Adair!" he said forthrightly. "I've heard a lot about you, all good," he said benevolently.

Trowbridge's handshake was weak and pudgy. Harvey was surprised at the fact his voice was very deep, his tone polished and with that slight accent that was not regional, but patrician. Still, the fellow was not at all suave. There were beads of perspiration dotting his forehead—the fat man's curse, for it was a cool October evening and the skin of his arms, neck and face was very white, and almost feminine in its seemingly hairless appearance. He was not dressed very handsomely at all—navy slacks, an undistinguished silver-buckled belt, and a white shirt open at the neck. Harvey was wearing a new bright blue, red, black and gray mohair plaid coat-sweater from Celli of Milan—when he removed it the label would show—a white shirt and black knit tie, charcoal-gray slacks, and black calf shoes. The sweater, though, was his proudest possession that night. It had a continental collar, smoked pearl buttons, and a full red silk lining, with a large white label.

Adair Trowbridge, after his initial greeting, stood wordless. Behind Harvey, Lois and her father had not yet made a move forward. Harvey knew Lois was probably all upset, probably completely misled as to Harvey's intentions this evening, but he would straighten it all out. It might be a little awkward at first, but somehow the sight of Trowbridge had given Harvey a booster shot of confidence. Trowbridge was in his late thirties, at least. Not that Harvey had any intention whatsoever of breaking up Trowbridge and Lois—not any more—but it made what he did have in mind seem all the more likely— the fact that Adair Trowbridge was such a colorless specimen. His picture in the *Tribune* had led Harvey to imagine he would be quite a bit grander than this sad chap with the receding hairline and protruding waistline.

He said to Trowbridge, "How are the ferns?"

Trowbridge smiled weakly, as Harvey continued to talk. Harvey said, "From the Latin hortus, we have garden and from the Latin cultura, we have cultivation. Horticulture." Harvey had never taken Latin in school; any Latin he knew he had learned himself, from reading the dictionary, and the words sounded very cultured to him. He was as proud of the Latin he knew as he was of the three or four words in Russian he knew. He continued talking to Adair, saying, "A very interesting hobby, photographing flowers and whatnot. How did you become interested, Adair?"

Trowbridge was glancing back at the Cutlers with an anxious expression, his hands fooling with a reel of movie film on the projector. He said, "My father was a gardener."

"Oh, well you've come a long way then. I suspect he's proud of you."

"I beg your pardon?"

"How many gardener's sons get their pictures in the Sunday *Tribune*?" Harvey said with a gentle smile.

"That wasn't what I meant," Trowbridge said. "Gardening was a pleasure of my father's."

"Oh. Not a living, eh?"

"No . . . not a living."

"I should have known from your name," said Harvey. "How many gardeners would name their sons Adair?"

Trowbridge said, "I have no idea."

"It's a funny name," said Harvey. "I looked it up. It

means 'from the ford by the oak trees.' I suppose you knew that."

"No."

"It's Celtic," Harvey said.

Trowbridge said nothing. Then Hayden Cutler cleared his throat in a portentous manner and stepped forward, Lois following a few paces behind.

Culter said, "I'm afraid you've interrupted us, Harvey. Adair was showing us some films of Venice which he took last summer."

"While I was in the neighborhood," Harvey said, "I thought I'd drop in and straighten out a few things."

"I wish you'd telephoned first," Cutler said. "We might have avoided embarrassment all the way around."

"You mean because Adair's here? I'm glad he's here, Mr. Cutler, sir. Look," Harvey smiled. "I have no ill feeling. I admit I was shocked. It was all very sudden, it seemed to me."

"I've known Adair for years and years," Lois said. "Haven't I, Daddy?"

"Oh, never mind. Never mind," said Harvey, "I'm resigned to it. That's the way the ball bounces."

"We know Adair very well," Cutler said, "and we don't know you very well at all, Harvey."

"All I want is a chance, sir," Harvey said brightly. "That's why I came by. There's no reason we can't all be good friends."

"Perhaps that's true," Cutler answered, "but none of our friends simply barge in on an evening. Please don't make it any more embarrassing, Harvey. We've been very patient, already."

"I don't have leprosy, you know, sir," Harvey chuckled. "Couldn't we all watch Adair's movies . . . Adair, you wouldn't mind, would you?" Harvey clamped an affectionate arm across Trowbridge's shoulders. "Bygones are bygones. Hmmm? I wasn't much of a threat at all, anyway," Harvey said generously. "I tried, but the best man won."

Trowbridge was not much of a talker.

Hayden Cutler said, "We have to ask you to leave, Harvey. I'm sorry, but you force me to be very blunt."

"But why must I leave? I'm really resigned to the whole thing, Mr. Cutler. Don't you believe that? Lois, don't you?"

Lois Cutler said, "I told you over the phone that I didn't want to see you any more, Harvey."

"But over the phone it was different. I was still upset. Look, Lois—Mr. Cutler—I've had time to think. You were perfectly right. I took too much for granted. It wasn't my fault. I mean, how was I to know Adair was abroad! Lois didn't even mention Adair. Not once." The unfairness of his plight glowed again in Harvey's heart like a little worm turning itself on again, and there was a slight quiver to his voice—a trembling in his insides. He started to complain more, but Cutler held up his hand. "Harvey," Cutler said, "Lois may have been to blame for not mentioning Adair, but she and Adair made up their minds only a week after he returned. All's fair in love and war, you know, and now it's up to you to do the decent thing. Fade away like the good old soldier who never dies. Fade away, boy . . . now. I'll walk you to the front door."

"Can't we all be friends anyway? Sir, I'd like your advice about entering business."

"This way, Harvey. Come along." Cutler had Plangman firmly by the arm.

Lois said, "Bon nuit, Monsieur."

"I think it's really rotten of you," said Harvey. "After all, I was doing the sporting thing, Lois."

"I told you over the phone, Harvey Plangman. And Daddy told you."

"Nice to have met you, Trowbridge," Harvey called over his shoulder. "We might have been good friends, if we'd been given the chance."

Trowbridge only nodded, without smiling.

At the door, Hayden Cutler said, "I wouldn't come back, Harvey. You know, you're only making a fool of yourself. Why do that?"

"Why do you dislike me so? That's what I can't get through my head, Mr. Cutler. Why, I gave you a birthday party. Now I'm not even welcome in your house."

"The birthday party you gave me was a great compliment to my daughter, Harvey."

"But that's what you don't understand, sir. I liked you too. I wasn't just interested in Lois."

"You weren't?"

"No, sir! You see, I'd like to consider myself a friend of the family. I'd like to feel I could drop in on you, and you could drop in on me. I don't think Adair's such a bad sort, at all. He has nothing to do with it, any more. I'm resigned, and I'd like to offer my friendship, sir."

"That's very nice, Harvey, but I'm a busy man, and I expect Lois and Adair don't want a third wheel around."

"Sir, I moved East for Lois. I bet you never knew that, sir."

"That was presumptuous, Harvey. Now, you're trying my patience."

"You want me to just leave. Just like that, is that it? And never come back?"

"I'm sorry. I'm afraid that's it."

"All right, sir, but Trowbridge will get it too. I know that. Lord, didn't I hear enough of your phone conversations together, with 'God bless me and God bless you,' and . . ."

"Get out, Plangman!"

Harvey felt himself being shoved. Then he was on the step outside, and the door was slammed shut.

He hurried down the walk to his car. He got in and drove toward town. Tears smarted in his eyes, and as he lit a cigarette, his hands trembled. When he passed the phone booth on the corner of Bridge Street in New Hope, he pulled over to the curb. A man named Axtel who was forty-three inherited two-hundred and fifty-one thousand dollars; he still knew the number without looking it up.

"Hello, Margaret," he might say. "I'd like to come and talk with you."

He stood in the phone booth, holding the dime in his hand. Mrs. Bowser, not Margaret—not Margaret until after he talked with her. After she trusted him and liked him. His heart was pounding; his mind busy manufacturing the fantasy:

". . . and do you see, Mrs. Bowser, I've helped him all I could. I've lent him money and given him a place to stay, but if you want my opinion, he's in much more serious difficulty than that of a man who's committed a crime. Yes, embezzlement is serious enough, Mrs. Bowser, but he's having a nervous breakdown. I should have realized that from the start, but I didn't know him at all, you see. It was just chance that our coats got mixed up in that gas station, and I felt sorry for him . . ."

"Harvey, please call me Margaret. I've grown to trust you. You seem almost like a son."

"Thank you, Margaret."

"What can we do about it?"

"For his own good, Margaret, I think we ought to turn him in. At the risk of our friendship—yours and mine—I have to speak honestly..."

"It's a hard decision to make. He's my husband."

"Would you think of me as a son? And I'll be by your side..."

"Thank you, Harvey."

"I grew to think of him as a father. You know, I even wrote him for advice from time to time. But I began to realize he was really seriously ill..."

"I'd like to repay you in some way."

"I don't want money. But if you'll let me be by your side..."

"Harvey, I have an idea. Why don't you come and live with us?"

He smiled. Something like that; something like that. He would figure it all out on his way there. He dropped the dime in the slot and dialed. He tried to remember what he had written in his letters to Bowser. He would have to get them back; he would have to get Margaret to agree to keep everything said between them confidential.

"I don't want to be an accessory, you know. I was only trying to help."

"Of course you were...."

A woman's voice answered. "Hello?"

"Hello, Mrs. Bowser?" he said.

"No, she isn't here. This is Edith Summers."

"When will Mrs. Bowser return, please?"

"She's in Nassau with her mother. I'm just here watering the plants, but I write her and..."

"No," said Harvey. "Never mind."

He walked down Main Street to the Logan Inn, and went to the bar.

"Hi!" he said to the bartender. "I'll have an Old Smuggler and water. Pretty quiet tonight, ah?"

There was only one couple in the place, a man and woman down at the other end of the bar. He should have sat closer to them, but it was too late now. He smiled at them, and they smiled back.

"Pretty quiet tonight," he repeated.

His hands were shaking, so that he had to wait a minute

before he could sip his drink without sloshing it on his new sweater. The sweater had cost him a hundred dollars. He had bought it at Leighton's in New York. He decided to take it off, fold it so that the Celli of Milan label showed, and place it on the bar.

He managed to raise the glass to his mouth and get a good gulp of the whisky. The couple at the end of the bar were talking together, and the bartender was working a crossword puzzle. He fought back tears. After a few minutes, he ordered another Old Smuggler and water. When the bartender served it, he said, "I guess not much happens around here after the summer season."

"Nice and quiet, the way I like it," the fellow said.

"That's the way I like it too!" said Harvey. "I was telling Adair just that, a little earlier this evening..." He looked down to see if his words registered with the people at the end of the bar. They were still talking together. He said to the bartender, "Adair Trowbridge, you know him?"

"Isn't he the fellow who takes pictures of flowers?"

"Yes, that's Adair!" Harvey said enthusiastically.

"I don't know him personally. I know he's got a place around here somewheres."

"A studio," said Harvey. "He's a fern man. Ferns are his specialty. Engaged to Lois Cutler. We're all friends."

"Umm hmm. Yeah, I know Lois and her dad."

"Great people!" said Harvey.

"Yeah, they're nice." The bartender started back to his puzzle. Harvey said, "May I buy you a drink?"

"Thanks, but I don't drink myself."

"Maybe I can buy them one," Harvey said, nodding at the people down at the end of the bar. They looked up and he smiled at them. "Drink?" he asked.

The man smiled back. "We're on our way home. Thanks anyway."

Harvey ordered another Old Smuggler and water. He could feel his knees shaking. He gulped half of it, and took the rest around the corner in the Logan, through the office to the phone booth.

"Hello?"—a man's voice.

"Mr. Cutler?"

"Yes."

"Harvey Plangman, sir."

"Yes."

"Please don't sound that way, and please don't hang up. What I said this evening was very rude, sir, and I apologize."

"All right, Plangman."

"You see, sir, I really think it's a fine thing to have strong family ties. Where would anyone be without them, sir, after all? And I meant it when I said I'd like to be a part of your family, because I need that very much, to be a part..."

There was the dial tone.

SEVENTEEN

CHRISSY SLAMMED her hand down hard at the fly on the table in the soda shop. "Damned bee!" she cried out. The spoon from her ice cream sailed onto the floor, chocolate drippings spotting the table, and she began to cry as the fly buzzed out of her reach.

"Honey, it wasn't a bee." Bunny said to her.

"She said damn, Mommy," Carla tugged at her mother's sweater. "Chrissy said damn, Mommy."

Battle tried comforting the baby, but Chrissy gave him a slap and wailed all the louder.

"Now you stop that," Battle said firmly, pointing his finger at her. "You stop it or you're getting a spanking."

"Won't top!"

"Oh, yes you will!" Battle threatened.

"Mommy, Chrissy said damn!" said Carla.

"Ray, there's no reason to yell at her like that!"

"Won't top!" Chrissy wailed.

"Chrissy said damn, Mommy, and that's naughty. I don't say damn."

"You just said it!" Battle said angrily.

"If you're out of patience, Ray, you can go on without us."

"Why aren't they trained? Why do they just carry on like wild Indians?"

"I don't say damn either!" Carla said angrily, pounding the table with her four-year-old fist. "You're not a nice man!"

"Just go on without us, Ray."

"Chuss go on out us," said Chrissy, pouting at him.

Battle sat there glumly. It was never any good when they went out, even when they were alone. Bunny was wiping the children's dirty faces with Kleenex. "It was your own idea to come here for ice cream," she said. "You just don't have any patience, Ray."

"Oh, and I suppose Banjo does."

"We like Banjo!" Carla said emphatically. "We like him, don't we, Mommy?"

"Yes, dear, but don't call him Banjo. It's Scott."

"We like Stot," said Chrissy, giving Battle a snide look.

Afterward, when Battle loaded them all into the second-
hand Ford he had purchased last week, Carla said, "And we
like Scott's car better too! We like to sit behind the buckets."

"Bucket seats," said Bunny. "Not buckets." She giggled.

"You see," Battle told her as he started the car, "that's
how they get that way. You just giggle at them and don't
bother correcting them."

"It's a harmless mistake. Buckets for bucket seats. Am I
supposed to punch her in the jaw for saying it?"

"I don't mean that. It's rude for Carla to say she likes
his car better. She has to learn respect, learn to control herself. It's just rude."

"Oh, piffle!"

"And I hate that expression. It's childish."

"What a lovely afternoon it's been with old Scrooge.
Thanks, Ray."

"I hope you enjoy your evening more," he said.

"Don't worry!"

"I hope bed is just great. You can start with *Gone With
The Wind* and work your way up to *Peyton Place!*"

Bunny shouted, "Haven't I told you that kind of talk in
front of the children is out, Ray? Let us out of the car!"

"Oh, stop dramatizing yourself!"

"You're not going to say things like that in front of the
children."

"Yes," Carla said from the back seat. "We're just little
girls!"

"Chuss go on out us," said Chrissy.

"We like Scott better!" Carla said.

"Stot better!" said Chrissy.

Bunny began giggling again. Ray pressed his foot down on
the gas and drove faster.

"What I want someday," Bunny said, "is a nice little
Triumph convertible to match my hair, with a bunny on the
door."

"What a noble ambition, Mrs. Carson."

"Well, I won't be driving a second-hand Ford when I'm
forty-two years old."

"No, you'll be too busy receiving curtain calls on Broadway, I suppose."

"Make fun of me all you want, Ray."

"And Banjo will be your leading man. Bunny and Banjo.
Lunt and Fontanne."

"Every time we go out it's like this," she said. "Every single time."

"I know it," Ray said. Then he reached for her hand. "I'm sorry."

"Thank you," she said.

They drove along in silence for awhile. As he turned on Wentwroth he said, "I love it the way you let things drop. I love that."

"Thank you, Ray."

"Can you come in for a minute? Do you have to go right upstairs?"

"I'll come in if Mother's home to take the kids," she said.

"We like Scott better, don't we, Mommy?" Carla said from the back seat.

Bunny said, "Don't say that, Carla. It's not nice."

"Is it worse than saying damn? Chrissy said 'damn.' "

"It's just as bad," said Bunny, "only it's different. Damn is an impolite word, and saying that you like someone else better, in front of a person, is an impolite feeling."

"What time is your date?" Ray asked.

"Seven."

"It's four now."

"I have to feed the kids. I can't stay long."

The letter was in his pocket. The advertisement he had answered ten days ago turned out to be one placed by a firm in Canada. They manufactured swimming pools and were expanding into the manufacture of home bomb shelters. The opening was for a personnel head to handle the hiring of franchise representatives for the United States. The applicant would be required to live in Toronto.

Battle had drafted a careful resumé. He listed the bulk of his experience with a defunct mayonnaise factory in upstate New York. The factory had been under surveillance at King & Clary with Robert Bowser handling the reports, and while it had been turned down as a likely investment, it had enjoyed a good reputation in its time; and Battle knew that the man who had headed the business was now retired in Spain. Battle had distorted the address of the man in his references, just enough to make it impossible for him to receive any letter of inquiry. He had an idea that the matter would not be pursued too persistently. Time was an important factor in the new business of survival equipment; every swimming pool company in the country would be adding the line before long. The Canadian firm had a unique design and the advantage of a new material, which was economical and easy to ship, but it would also be easily imitated once the boom was in full swing. Battle had listed the vice-president of the defunct mayonnaise corporation as Harvey Plangman. He had already received and answered a letter of inquiry about Battle. The letter had been mailed to 702. Battle had rented a P.O. box in St. Louis for his own correspondence. As Plangman, he had written to the Canadian firm that he thought Battle was a sales executive in St. Louis now, adding that any establishment would be lucky to have a man of Raymond Battle's caliber.

The letter Battle had in his pocket was an invitation to fly to Toronto for an interview, a very reassuring invitation that all but guaranteed Battle the position.

It was the third and only promising response Battle had received from the various advertisements he had answered. He had been searching through *The New York Times,* the *Kansas City Star,* the *Wall Street Journal,* and other newspapers, for the past two weeks. He had looked specifically for opportunities in Canada and Mexico. He had gone about St. Louis and Columbia and Kansas City acquiring various pieces of indentification as Raymond Battle. A bank account in Kansas City, a charge account in St. Louis, and now his wallet contained three or four cards listing that name. At a post office in Jefferson City one afternoon, he had seen a Wanted bill with a picture of Robert Bowser glaring out at him like a bored old owl. He had studied the picture carefully. It was almost as though he were looking at a photograph of a stranger. He was amused to see that it was a Bachrach portrait, with Wanted For Embezzlement printed where the Bachrach credit would normally be. Bowser looked much older than Battle, slightly formidable and very tired. Battle wore the contact lenses full time now. He had put on some weight, and his face was no longer as gaunt as Bowser's ——but there was a more important difference. Battle tried to pinpoint it, but he could not; he only knew Bowser would hate a Bunny Carson. She would be the sort that had always irritated Bowser——a gum-chewing waitress who forgot his order, a servant who played the radio too loudly, a secretary at King & Clary who did her nails at her desk. No, Battle was wrong——Bowser would not hate her. He would simply dismiss her from his mind. He would be what Battle had not been able to be——indifferent to her.

Raymond Battle for the past two weeks had drowned in feelings of hot and high and terribly intense happiness, only to be rung out immediately afterward by his own nearly morbid self-hatred. It was not morbid in any true sense of helpless despair, for he fought off his demons in very practical ways: he made his plans. He told himself he was finding a way to get out and get hold of himself again and he would whistle down the halls, a slight but noticeably brave spring to his step, his head held high, his resolve to stay away from her firm. He considered Bunny a necessary but despicable ingredient in this soup of confusion which Plangman's plot had thrust him into. Without her, he might very well have wallowed in the soup. He might have gone on practicing the same little habits of picayune gratification (the TV and the tea timed with the toast, the tiny, foolish ways of one alone) week after week, month after month, feeling bewildered and sorry for himself, and yes, even grateful that his fate was out of his hands. But this terrible physical involvement with someone else made him miss freedom and want it again. There was nothing like the thorough dissipation of meaningless sensuality to force the sensation of remorse, and ultimately, to force him again to think. First, he would get out from under her clutches. Step by step, step by step; it would all take time. Meanwhile, he told himself, meanwhile he would have nothing to do with her.

He could not stand it, seeing himself the way she made him, so that he was jealous of a type like Banjo.

"Not jealous, Bunny," he would tell her. "It isn't that. But shocked that you haven't any more ego than that—to accept someone like him, so beneath you. His hair down his back, and did you ever hear him speak intelligently?"

"You're right," she would say.

"Of course I am. You know I'm not a moralist—morals haven't anything to do with it. You're on your own, we both know that, but there are Chrissy and Carla to consider. He's a very low type to have around your home."

"You're right."

"Now, if it were a decent chap—one of the fraternity boys or someone with a background that amounted to something. I'm not a snob, but . . ."

"He doesn't believe in fraternities."

"Oh, he just can't get in one. Do you see the fraternity boys running around with their hair down their backs?"

"You're right. I told him his hair looks silly."

"He won't listen. He's one of these Bohemians!"

"I like Bohemians, Ray!"

"Sure. Yes, and so do I. But don't cheapen yourself by becoming overly attached. Don't you see what I mean? You know I want the best for you. I don't want to see you getting a bad reputation. It's not dignified, you know. You have to think of that. There's Chrissy and Carla to consider. Someday you'll want to marry a decent man; never mind all this about wanting to be an actress, Bunny. You'll want to marry someone substantial. That's it—someone substantial. I wouldn't say a word, if you'd pick someone substantial."

"I know what you're saying is right."

He would carry on and on like that, only to wake up the next day and remember his attacks of womanish hysteria with revulsion—for her and himself. And she, never one to think quickly, would mull it over and compound his self-revulsion by appearing in his place next day just long enough to let him have it.

"Who are you anyway," she would shout. "You fix the johns around here, for God's sake! Who are you to look down on anyone?" she would hammer away at him. "You're forty-two and what did you amount to? If you're not careful, your goddam eyes fall out on the rug!"

Then there was the naked rage spilling open between them, with its ugly name-calling and shouting hatred, and he would stand amazed at the red homeliness of her face as she screamed at him, and at his own shrill sounds, and at the spectacle of himself come to this, wanting this. He would feel lecherous, as he often felt when they were out somewhere alone together and he knew the college boys looked at her, and then at him. It was always bad when they went out; still, he would insist on it, because he felt she knew it was bad, and each time he set out to remove that obstacle—and each time it was there again.

Once he said to her, when they were in bed, where it was always easy to talk and things were good between them, "Why don't you ever say you love me?"

"Oh, Ray!"

"Well, it's a good question. You always say 'Thank you', but you don't say that you love me."

"I can't."

"Why not?"

"I love you, but I can't say it."

"You just did. You can say it that way, but not after I say it."

"I just can't. I just don't ever. Not with anyone."

"Why? Why can't you with me?"

"I can't."

"You could. You could."

"Ray, don't pick on me again," and she began to cry that way she had of crying that absolutely turned his stomach with disgust. The first time he ever heard it, he thought she was fooling. It was a child's way of crying, a horrible wahhhhh sound, and she would pound her sides with her fists and just go wahhh! wahhh! O-wahhhh!

He had left her that time with another promise to himself never to go back, and he had made himself some tea on his stove downstairs, and damned himself for his asinine conversation with her about why she could not say she loved him.

It was being such a goddamed fool that he was getting away from, and each time his resolve was firmer.

Of course he would break, and the break would come quite suddenly in the midst of some perfectly ordinary task—scrambling his breakfast eggs, cleaning out his tub—just at a time when he would feel a confident incredulousness at the very fact of his whole involvement with her. How had it ever happened? He would shake his head in amazement—perfectly wretched little hoyden, empty as an ant—and he would daydream about working again at the things he was good at and knew. Random ideas and memories came back to his mind: "the merger agreement provides for an exchange of 199,560 shares of a new $2.125 cumulative preferred stock of . . ." and then he would stand helpless while the pulling apart began inside him, finally recognizing the symptom; then the accompanying flood of panic while everything crumbled and he knew where he was really headed.

"Oh," she would say, "it's you back."

Or she wouldn't say anything, depending on her mood, but she would cry in that detestable way again and hang on to him tightly, the way he had dreamed of her doing when he was alone.

Now, however, he had the letter. It was in his pocket. He would have to leave without telling her where he was going, without any notice to her that he was planning to leave. He could not chance anyone's knowing his plans. In four days, he would be cleared out of 702 Wentwroth.

She left the children with Mrs. Hill after they got back to the house. He knew she was going to arrange something when he took her hand in the car. He knew too that there was nothing physical between Banjo and Bunny. "We just neck," she had told him once; God, what an impossible word "neck" was! Before this whole thing had happened to him, he had never known anyone who used the word. Well, there you were! He supposed after he left they would probably . . . but he refused to entertain any thoughts about what she would do once he was gone. It would be no concern of his. He felt sad with that knowledge. He made love to her in his apartment that afternoon with a melancholy mood—but his sadness was mixed with relief and pity for her. He knew it was good for her when they were together. Once, up in 3, he had peeked into a recent diary of hers and seen an entry which said, "Me again. R. is the b.l. I ever had, but the b! Nite Nite." He was always tickled by her inclination to camouflage her more personal activities. Once, they had eaten out at a restaurant in Columbia and their table was squeezed next to someone else's; everything they said could be overheard. Bunny had leaned forward at one point and said to Battle, "Do you think anyone in here knows we're s.l.e.e.p.i.n.g. together?" Battle had roared with laughter and answered, "Not unless they can s.p.e.l.l."

While she was putting her clothes back on, Battle watched her wistfully. Margaret had always been ashamed to walk about naked. There was something contagious about such an attitude. Bowser too had always covered himself. He liked the way Bunny did it—not matter-of-factly—she was aware she was pretty and she did not let herself assume any postures which would detract from that idea, but she was neither self-conscious nor exhibitionistic, and it was the same way in bed. Oddly enough, Margaret was a bit exhibitionistic in bed; things were always a little overdone with Margaret. It was her extravagance again; it was the same way she shopped. She did not really need anything; it was just that when you shopped, you shopped.

"Scott and I are going to a drive-in," said Bunny, buttoning her blouse. "Out by the Hinkson."

"Well, have a good time." He admired the sound of generosity and permissiveness in his voice. He meant it; why shouldn't he?

"Thanks. I really like Scott."

"I'm just sorry it's someone like Scott. I think you deserve better, that's all."

"At least he's my own age."

"Umm hmmm."

"He could have gotten into a fraternity. I asked him. He was rushed by ATO and Lambda Chi."

"Sure."

"Well, he was, Ray."

Battle got off the bed and walked across, turned her around and kissed her. "I love you, Bunny," he said. "Have a good time tonight. I mean that."

"Thank you," she said. "I'm really looking forward to it."

"Good."

"Bye, Ray. See you tomorrow some time."

"Bye!" he said. He smiled and blew her a kiss. She had that strange little pinched expression on her face as she went out the door. Poor kid; she was beginning to fall hard.

He made himself a lamb chop and a baked potato, and ate it in front of the TV, not concentrating very much on the news program being shown. He knew all her tricks now. One day last week when he had gone up to 3 at the usual time, she had left an unfinished letter on her desk.

"Dearest," it began, "How I have missed you, my love, thinking of you day and night."

He had said, "Who's 'Dearest'?"

"No one you know," she had answered. He saw her suppress a smile of self-satisfaction, and he had known instantly the letter was a plant, put there for his benefit. Her transparencies touched him at the same time they amused him—and sometimes, less and less lately, he was trapped by them, and they would be the cause of another fierce argument. If it was not Banjo she used to taunt him, it was Professor Cameron, her speech teacher, or Mr. Blaststein, her drama teacher—any fool she could think of to name. For Bunny, there was no such thing as an ordinary day, to hear her recount it. This one said something provocative and that one had a certain look; Battle caught on to it after awhile. God, how he could predict her. That afternoon after their love-making he had been sitting there watching her and wondering just how close he could come to predicting her first sentence after she got out of bed. He had bet on: "Scott's picking me up at eight."

"Scott and I are going to a drive-in," she'd said instead.

Battle chuckled and cut up more pieces of the lamb chop.
He supposed all women's games were a bit contagious; after
all, he had gone along with a lot of it. He had allowed himself to be carried away with bursts of temper, and with the
violent aftermath of making up in bed. Sometimes when
they were making up in bed that way, he had a perfect picture
of how foolish he looked throughout the whole maneuver,
and he would say to himself, "Battle, what an ass you really
are! Ass! Ass! Silly ass!"

Then too, he felt slightly repelled by the way she could
kid herself at these times, and when she was hanging to him
tightly in ecstasy, he was often unable to stop thinking, "What
a stupid, empty little bitch you are!" At those times, there
was always something clumsy and primeval about whatever
position they were in, and he had weird sights to contend
with on the screen of his inner mind, as well as the direction of
their communion. Sometimes he would see the brutal, ugly,
figures of human dissipation as Goya had painted them in his
grotesque *Caprichos;* sometimes he would see old four-eyed
Robert Bowser back in his solarium at New Hope, that night
he had read the letter from Gertrude in Plangman's wallet.
He would see his asinine face taking it all in with that loath-
some innocence which was the beginning of this lechery.
Battle had read once, in one of Graham Greene's novels,
that innocence was like a dumb leper who had lost his bell.

He pushed his plate away and stuffed his pipe, put his feet
up on the hassock, and lit the tobacco in the pipe. Still, he
would have good memories too. A couple of nights they had
gotten very pleasantly high together and talked and talked
about all sorts of nonsense she was interested in——that Triumph
convertible she wanted to match the color of her hair, with a
bunny on the door. She had all sorts of things with bunnies
on them. Raymond Battle laughed aloud. Handkerchiefs with
bunnies on them, coffee mugs with bunnies on them, com-
pacts, scarves, lipstick tubes. She knew it irritated him when
she carried on about wanting the Triumph; she had mentioned
it again that afternoon. But at times, when they were high,
she talked about it, not to irritate him, but because she really
did want it, and he listened to her, his good taste anesthetized
by the liquor, and he liked listening.

"It would make me feel special to have that car," she would
say.

"Why do you need to feel special?"

"Because I'm not, Ray."

That answer always made him giggle the same way she did. They would both giggle and kiss, and he felt pretty happy.

Battle changed the channel to a detective series, though he was not in the mood at all for the television tonight. He had never told her very much about himself, naturally. Knowing her partiality for the dramatic, he had mumbled something once about his immense bereavement making it impossible for him to talk about his past. He was sorry he was unable to trust her and tell her the whole thing. To this day, he had no idea whatsoever of how Margaret had taken all of it; simply none. But he knew Bunny. Bunny would be delighted with the idea of protecting him. At the same time she would hold it over his head in every single argument, threatening to expose him, and calling him robber, thief, and thug until she was red in the neck and nearly ready to turn course, and head back in the direction of some soft place to make it all up to him.

He supposed some day he would laugh at it all. Some day, he would look up from a column of figures, or a company report of some sort, and he would remember and his lips would tip in that curious small grin of long ago, and he would hear her voice say, "Thank you," that special way.

A week ago, on an evening when Mrs. Hill was taking the children to a carnival, he and Bunny had planned dinner together at his place. Bunny had said, "We can have one of our evenings, Ray. Lots of drinks before dinner, something very yummy to eat, with a bottle of wine——a brandy apiece afterwards, and then make love like mad. Hmmm?"

He had never minded the fact she did not like to cook. There were so many things she had never tasted; he liked making them for her. He liked her enthusiasm, and the fact she was not finicky or static in her preferences. He had done the shopping late that afternoon, buying a huge amount of food for a very complicated Paella Valenciana. Margaret loved paella too, but it was not the same to eat something with Margaret, whether she loved it or not. She was always remarking, "They used more saffron in that place in Madrid, remember, Robert. I think it was better." Or, "Is the rice right? It seems undercooked, doesn't it, Robert?" He had bought sausage and oysters and lobster and chicken and clams for the dish, and a bottle of Soave, and he was hurrying along College Avenue with his arms full of the packages, humming to himself, and liking the fact Bunny was already in his apartment, making the cold martinis. It was a day when he really did love her (not all days were like that, by any means), and he liked making love with her on such days. He liked having dinner with her beforehand—and lots of, too many, drinks. Bunny understood about having too many drinks before dinner; sometimes it was just the thing to do—but it had always made Margaret either nervous or ill to have more than three before dinner. And toward the end, when Mother Franklin was living with them, it meant that Mother Franklin would have too many too, and she would either dance around lifting her skirts too high, in that depressing way that threw a wrench in the evening, or she would stagger off to the back porch and sob about no one loving her and refuse to eat. Battle hurried along College Avenue with his heart beating gaily, and his spirits soaring—just something simple and wonderful to look forward to. At the corner of College and Crumson, before he turned into Wentwroth, he had noticed the sermon board in front of the Baptist Church. Contained behind the glass was a block of three words, no more. The message said: Enter Into Joy.

He would probably remember that someday too, someday far off—he would remember how he felt when he saw those words. It was a good thing for a man to have a particular day which he could remember in glorious detail, an ordinary and not particularly special day—not a wedding day or a day when a war ended or a day when something big happened—but just a simple day when he felt as though everything was just perfect.

Battle gave up watching television after he had smoked his pipe. He got out a piece of paper and a ballpoint and began making a list of things to do during the next four days. There was not so much to do, but what there was to be accomplished, had to be taken care of very carefully. He would have to notify Mrs. Plangman that he was going to be out of town for a few days, just in case she dropped by and became alarmed at his absence. He planned to tell Bunny the same thing. He would write his usual letter to Plangman (though Plangman's last letter asked for no advice, but ranted on about the phony first names some people had, and how Plangman was glad Bowser hadn't been named something like Adair or Lake. Battle could not make head or tail of it. He suspected Plangman was drunk when he wrote it) and he would leave behind enough things to make it look as though he were returning. There was not much he wanted to take anyway; certainly not the clothes he had been wearing around Columbia. He would need new clothes. He supposed he would buy them in St. Louis before his plane left.

He walked about thinking of what he would take with him. His shaving equipment and a few ties, shoes, socks, and not much else. He had a snapshot of Bunny and the kids he would take. On the other hand, he wouldn't take it. Why should he?

He looked at his watch and saw that it was after ten. She would probably not be home for another hour—perhaps later. He turned on the television again, filled his pipe again, and watched a drama about Berlin. In the midst of it, he chuckled, imagining himself married to someone like Bunny. The first thing he would do would be discipline those children. Lordgod, they needed a father, that was certain. He thought of Chrissy, his favorite, and the most difficult. In the ice cream shop that afternoon, he had suggested to Chrissy that she try some other flavor besides chocolate. She always had chocolate; she had never tasted any other kind.

"Try something new," he had said.

She had stared at him, while he rattled off the names: strawberry, orange, coconut-peach, vanilla. Her wide blue eyes had no expression in them. Finally Battle had said, "We'll have vanilla, okay?" No answer. "Vanilla it is," said Battle. Just as he gave the order to the waitress, Chrissy slammed the table with both her fists and screamed out: "I will not have manilla!"

She had then socked Battle in the chest with her fist and yelled, "I don't like manilla! It's what I hate!"

She had had her usual chocolate. Battle remembered an evening back with Mother Franklin, when he had absentmindedly stirred the marshmallow in her hot chocolate, and the old woman had screamed, "Don't stir it!" He supposed someday, some poor man would . . . but all Chrissy needed was a little discipline . . . His watch said eleven on the dot.

Battle got up and walked out into the hall. Down at the end, he peeked through the curtains. There was no car out front. He walked back, and switched channels to the late show. He supposed half the people in Columbia thought he was the children's grandfather, and Bunny, his daughter. He got up and walked into the bathroom, and looked at himself in the mirror. His back teeth were bad; he supposed when he got to a dentist up in Toronto, he would have to cope with a bridge of some sort. She once said he had enough gold in his mouth to make a bracelet for her. It was when she was lying on top of him, before they had made love. She was the most indelicate damn little bitch he could ever imagine. At a time like that, picking out something like that—and he, he supposed, was supposed to lie there with visions of his ugly gaping gold-jammed jaw and feel romantic. Very typical— the whole damn thing was shoddy—eleven-thirty.

He walked back out to the end of the hall and looked again through the curtains. No car. He walked back. He sat down and watched an old movie with Jane Withers in it. Of the $15,000, he had ten left—$9,899.03. He brought his hands up and sank his face into his palms. Of course, he would miss her for a little while, that was only natural. It was funny that he had not really missed Margaret once. He had been stunned with loneliness in the beginning, before he had settled in at 702, but never once had he thought of Margaret's hand on him to soothe him, nor her voice saying anything to comfort him. He had expected that he would miss her. He didn't —he looked at his watch again, and now he was beginning to perspire. She had often come in much later than twelve when she was with him; Banjo probably had her at some moldy old student hangout drinking beer. Battle always hated going to the student places with her. He always felt miscast, and then, in turn, downcast—it was just never any good when they were out together.

At ten after one he heard the car. He had left his door ajar, and he heard the squeal of brakes as the car stopped short in front of 702. Battle got up and went down the hall rapidly, opened the door, and went directly to the side of the car where Bunny sat.

"Why, Ray? What are you . . ."

"You'd better come inside," he said. "It's important."

"The children?"

"Yes, the children," said Battle crazily. His heart was pounding, and as Banjo started to get out his side, Battle pushed him back in. He barked. "This isn't for you, Scott. You'd better get home."

"What is it?"

"We don't have time!" Battle shouted. Bunny was running ahead, and somehow, Battle had convinced the guitar-player. Almost dutifully he saluted Battle with a grave expression, and drove off looking very worried. Battle ran in the house, up the stairs to the second landing, where he caught her.

"What is it?" her eyes were terrified. "Let me get to them . . ."

"The children are all right," he said. "I was lying."

"You what?"

"I was lying," he said. "I wanted you to come inside!"

"Why—you—damn, damn you, Ray, goddam . . ."

He clamped his hand over her mouth. He said, "Shut up and listen to me. I want to marry you."

She stopped struggling. He dropped his hand. "I want to marry you," he said. "I have a job in Canada. An important one. We'll take Chrissy and Carla, and go to Toronto. You can have your Triumph with the bunny on it and any other damn thing you want."

"Ray!" Her face began to take the shape it did before she began crying in that terrible way.

"Jesus, don't cry," he said. "Don't make that horrible noise!"

"You want to marry me? Oh, Ray!" She grabbed him around the neck with such strength he thought she would topple him over and down the flight of stairs. She began to cry, trying not to, but there it was. In between those monstrous sounds she was burping, "I l-l-love you, Ray. I really and honestly l-love you."

"I love you too," he said.

"Th-thank you."

"I can't be without you," he said. He heard Professor Bullard's door open behind him; he could feel the old man's eyes on the back of his neck.

"Oh, Ray, why didn't you tell me before this?" she was sobbing.

Bullard said, "I had a thing to say, but I will fit it in with some better time. King John. Act III." He shut his door.

"Will you marry me, Bunny?" said Battle.

"Oh, natch! Natch!"

"Come down to my place," said Battle. "We've got a lot to talk about."

"Let me check the kids first and change. Then I'll be down."

"Hurry!" he said.

He took the stairs by twos, laughing. Why not? He would work it all out! Other men had begun again, and he could. Raymond Battle, and family. He would trust her, tell her everything and trust her; why not? Oh God, she would throw it up at him at every turn, he knew that. He gave his door a smart push with his shoe and sailed in, swinging his arms happily. It was enough for a start. $9,899.03. Plenty. He ran into the kitchen and got out the bottle of bourbon from under the sink. He set out two glasses on a tray and broke ice in the refrigerator. He felt wildly happy, grinning with it and rushing about the small kitchen. "I love you, I love you, I love you!" he said aloud, and he slapped his hands together, laughing. He carried the tray into the living room, and set it grandly on the coffee table, rushed back to the kitchen to look for cheese and crackers. "I love you, I adore you, I'm mad about you," he said. He giggled and saluted his reflection in the mirror. "Here's to Raymond Battle," he said.

At the gentle rapping on his door, he flew across and flung it open.

"Sursum corda!" Harvey Plangman said.

EIGHTEEN

HARVEY PLANGMAN stepped inside. He set down a small pigskin suitcase.

He smiled at Battle. "Was für gute Nachstisch konnen Sie mir geben, nicht dick machende?" he said.

Battle simply stared at him.

"That means: what good non-fattening dessert do you recommend? Oh, I'm very good at German these days. I was going to drop out of my class, because I wasn't meeting any friends in it, but then," he pulled off his suede gloves and unbuttoned his sports coat, "I decided that if I didn't go to my German class, I wouldn't have any contact with anyone. Not a soul. Are you lonesome too, Mr. B.?" He flopped into the easy chair before the television set. "Ich bin am Ende," he said, "It means, I'm lost. How about you, Mr. B.?"

Battle leaned against the door, listening for Bunny's steps. He said, "What are you doing here?"

"I came to visit. A little surprise, hmm?"

"I have to go upstairs a moment, Plangman."

"At this hour? I thought you'd be all tucked in, y'know."

"Well, normally, but one of the tenants needs—a light bulb." Battle ran into the kitchen and produced one from the cabinet. "I'm going to take this upstairs and give it to the tenant. I'll be right back."

"I'll be waiting, sir."

Battle met Bunny, just as she was leaving 3. She was wearing a thin blue nightie with a bathrobe thrown over it, and fur slippers. She was giggling, and she caught onto him and danced him once around in the hallway, while he pulled to be free. She was giggling and jabbering, "I told Mother we're getting married, Ray, and guess what! Banjo called, worried 'natch about what'd happened, and I just hung up on him, just dropped the . . ."

He shook her, unable to control his impatience, and his fear. "Something's happened," he said. "You can't come

159

downstairs now, Bunny. Someone's come from out-of-town, a business colleague. I'll explain tomorrow, but..."

"Business colleague?" she said. "Since when?"

"I told you about the Canadian job. I can't see you tonight, that's all! Go back inside, and we'll have breakfast tomorrow. I'll come up early."

"Ray, I got all yummied up in my new..." She was opening her robe to show him, and he took her hands roughly and pulled the robe closed.

"There isn't time, Bunny! Here, take this thing," thrusting the light bulb at her. "I'll explain it all tomorrow."

"Are you off your rocker, Ray?"

"Will you please do what I tell you to?"

"Do you still want to marry me?"

"Yes!" He was nearly shouting. "Please go back inside!"

"All right, Ray," she said. She was very peeved, the red color coming to her neck. She turned around and shut the door without another word. Battle ran back downstairs. In the living room, Plangman had poured himself a drink.

"You sure you weren't expecting me, Mr. B.?"

"You know I wasn't."

"A tray with two glasses all set up—I'm disappointed. I thought perhaps we were operating on the same wave length, and you had some sort of psychic knowledge I was on my way here."

"What do you want, Plangman?"

"So many things, really." He lit a cigarette, exhaled and leaned back in the chair, smiling crookedly at Battle. "You know," he said, "I'm not surprised any more at the amount you stole from King & Clary. I used to think $100,000 was a fantastic amount, but it's really chicken feed, isn't it? Money goes very quickly, doesn't it?"

"You're broke. That's it."

"I have one thousand dollars cash, right to the button, Mr. B. But that's broke by your standards, isn't it?"

"Where did the money go?"

"Ha! Ha! Don't you see the irony of your asking *me* that? Weren't you the one who claimed you had nothing to show for all you stole? You didn't spend it on liquor, gambling, other women—none of that. It just went, wouldn't you say? Well, so did mine go, sir. I spent it trying to buy my way in, I suppose you'd say. You're probably laughing at me, hmmm? It's obvious by now, isn't it, that you were right? I couldn't buy my way in."

"I'm not laughing. I'm sorry to hear it."

"You're sorry I'm back, aren't you? That's what you're sorry about."

"I won't deny it."

"No, I wouldn't if I were you either. You've been fairly level with me; outwardly, at any rate. I liked you, you know. You never irritated me the way your kind usually does. I suppose it was because I had you in a very vulnerable position, and you had no choice but to cooperate with me—but I genuinely liked you, Bowser. Only once did you behave the way your kind does. Do you remember when that was?"

Battle sighed and poured himself a drink.

Plangman sipped his own drink and said, "Back at the Black Bass, during our first interview. I said I was going to buy a Garbieri Canterbury belt, and you smirked. Remember?"

"No," said Battle. "I don't."

"Oh, yes, you smirked. Never mind though, I'm used to it. Adair Trowbridge pulled the same thing on me. By the by, Lois is marrying him, or at least they're engaged. My personal theory is that they'll have a very long engagement. I don't think Trowbridge can even get it up, and I think Hayden Cutler knows it, and that's why he likes Trowbridge. But that's another story. Apropos de rien, how come your parents named you Robert? Isn't that a rather insipid name? I mean, it must have looked insipid in your wedding announcement in *The Times,* with all the rest of your kind having those tra la la names: Adair, Foster, Haines, Justin, Searle. Robert is such a pukey name, don't you think?" He was pulling off his jacket, and arranging it over the back of the armchair. "Robert—tch! tch! Anyway, Adair Trowbridge smirked at me too. Some days after their engagement was published in *The Times*, I called on him. He raises ferns, by the by—you know the type? He's just as precious as a silver butter warmer from Tiffany. 'Plangman,' he says to me, 'you're something of a nuisance.' And he smirked, you know the type?"

"I'm afraid not," said Battle.

"He's your kind. I don't mean that you're like him, because in my opinion he's a limp-wrist, but he's of your class, Bowser. I mean, he's one of your gang, you know. Part of the old crowd. Superior. So screwing tra la la above it all, wouldn't you say? I mean, I'm just a worm or

something to your kind. Oh, you know I'm out there somewhere in the dirt—and on those nasty rainy days when
we worms are all hanging about on the sidewalks, you have
to step over us—but for the most part, you don't have to
have much to do with us worms, wouldn't you say?"

"I'm sorry things didn't work out, Plangman. I won't
say I told you so."

"Are you really sorry, Bowser?"

"Sorry enough. What are your plans?"

"We'll get to that in good time. I'm an admitted failure,
sir. I've been humiliated by some of the finest people in
the East. Hayden Cutler threatened to call the police if I
phoned again. Has anything like that happened to you, sir?"

"No, I can't say it has."

"I didn't think so. Your kind makes out, no matter what.
Apropos de rien, Monsieur, your wife is vacationing in Nassau with your mother-in-law. Been there for weeks! You
see how it goes, Mr. B? Nothing really affects your kind.
You embezzle $100,000 and go scot free, and they hop off
to Nassau, hmm? Would you say that was fair?"

Battle stuffed his pipe and struck a match to it, letting
Plangman rave on.

"But perhaps you've been lonesome, hmm, Bowser?"

"Perhaps. Yes."

"Have you? No one to talk to and all that?"

"Sort of lonesome, yes."

"Of course, you were free to come and go. By the way,
you look very well. I can't even tell you're wearing the
lenses. You don't look at all like Bowser." He poured himself more bourbon, stubbed out his cigarette in the ashtray.
"Even if you did look like Bowser, you still wouldn't have
much trouble. There hasn't been anything in the newspapers
for months. Not anything! I mean, it's just as though you
never existed—never stole $100,000, never disappeared into
thin air—just never existed."

"The police are working on it, Plangman. Don't worry.
I'll get it soon enough. Is that what you want?"

"I just want to know why your kind has everything so
soft, Bowser? Why would you say that is?"

"I don't think it is. There's a matter of initiative . . . But
there's no point to our discussing it. We'll never agree."

"Ah, initiative—that marvelous juice bubbling away inside of your kind. Know-how, hmm? Initiative. Are you
born with it?"

"What exactly do you want, Plangman?"

"I'd like initiative. I just don't know how to go about getting it. I never did. I'm not very good at initiative—not the way you are. I mean, figure it out. I don't have the initiative to get a job at King & Clary, or any place like that. Now, it stands to reason that if I don't have the initiative for that, then with or without initiative, I could never embezzle $100,000. I could get chicken-feed out of some cash register, or I could risk my life holding up a bank, maybe, but it's the rich who get richer. I wonder who said that? I'd bet my last thousand it was a rich man."

"What do you want, Plangman? Why did you come here?"

"You had plenty of initiative since I set you up here. Right?"

"What do you mean?"

"I mean, you have a woman, don't you? I hear she's my age. A pretty redheaded widow, ah, Bowser? My mother, by the by, is the worst gossip in the state of Missouri. A pretty redheaded widow, hmmm? And my God, Bowser, she lives right upstairs. Now that's initiative! So is running out of here with a light bulb, so you could warn her not to come down. Ha! Ha! Oh, Bowser, I really honest-to-God envy your kind. Even in hell you'd know all the right people, wouldn't you? Don't you just know your kind has probably found a way to make hell cooler for themselves? A redheaded widow right upstairs. I want to met her, Bowser. That's one thing I want, since you ask."

"And what else?"

"You see, Mr. Battle-Bowser, my friend, I've been alone a lot lately. Oh, not by choice—not my choice, anyway, but everyone else's. You'd think I had leprosy. I'm not kidding. Wait—let me tell you this. The other night in the St. Regis, I tried to strike up a conversation with this couple. Now, I mean a simple, goddam social conversation. Nothing in it for me! Well, sir, they moved. Picked up their drinks and moved. Has that ever happened to you, sir?"

"They probably thought you were—oh—horning in, or something, Plangman. You just don't walk up and talk to people."

"Don't give me that, sir. You could. I know you could. It's just me. Me and people like me. Worms. I've been thinking a lot about it lately. I moved you know—no, you didn't know. I was going to write. My sublet was up, so I moved to a hotel. It's a little friendlier, y'know? Going up and down in the elevator with lots of people—and the bar downstairs and all. People learn your name in a hotel too. "Want a shot?" He poured himself and Battle some whisky. "So I moved to the Dorset, Bowser. I went to the P.O. to file a change-of-address card, and it dawned on me that I'd never filed one at the Columbia P.O. Oh, I know you've been very good about forwarding what little mail a worm gets, but I got to thinking, sir. It isn't a good idea to have you forwarding my mail. It sort of establishes an intimacy between us, in the eyes of other people. Your handwriting on the letters and all. I got to thinking it might be used to establish the fact I'm an accessory to your little crime, and with my luck, sir, wouldn't it be like them to get me and not you? I mean, suppose something happened to you—you could drop dead or something—I'd still be an accessory. By the by, I want all my letters back."

"I didn't save them."

"I'll look around good to be sure."

"Don't worry. I don't want our intimacy established either, in the eyes of other people."

"Because I'm not good enough, hmmm?"

Battle sighed and didn't answer.

"To get back to my little story, sir," said Plangman, sipping the bourbon, lighting another cigarette. "You can imagine my surprise when the Columbia P.O. forwarded a letter from Toronto. It was a form letter, Bowser, thanking me for my cooperation in sending information on Raymond Battle, and requesting me to suggest his salary range . . . want another shot of your bourbon? You look as though you could use a stiff one along about now."

"No, thanks. So now you know that too."

"Yes, now I know that too. Oh, I admire you for it. I've always admired you people. I suppose that's the story of my life, wouldn't you say?"

"And what do you plan to do about it?"

"I haven't decided. Oh, money's part of it, naturally. I figure that you have at least $30,000 to $40,000 on you. I was going to get to that eventually, but since I got this strange letter in the mail, I realized I had to speed up things a bit."

"There's nowhere near that sum, Plangman. You're just dreaming if . . ."

Plangman waved away Battle's words. "We won't talk

about it now. I'd like to meet your woman, Bowser. Does she know anything?"

"No."

"Good. She doesn't know who you really are, hmmm?"

"No."

"Just you and I know—good. Can't we ask her down for a drink?"

"It's nearly two in the morning, Plangman."

"That late, is it? Well . . . Oh, you don't have to worry, I won't expose you. There wouldn't be any point in it. I just want to see her. It always intrigues me the way you people operate. Is she pretty? Never mind, Mither wrote that she was. And my age about, hmmm?"

"About."

"So I'll just visit with you for a few days," said Plangman, "and we'll see what we'll see. I ought to call Mother and say hello. She stays up quite late. We're not really very close, but we go through the motions, you see. Even she prefers your kind. Did you ever go over to the House?"

"No."

"Oh, it's very grand—very grand." He poured himself another shot. "I'm hungry, Bowser," he said. "How about a sandwich, hmmm?"

"A sandwich," Battle agreed, sighing. He got up and walked into the kitchen.

From the other room, Plangman was carrying on. "I was getting bored in New York anyway. I would have come back eventually. Do you know I might change my name? I might. Legally. I was thinking I might change my name and have my face fixed. It's my chin, in particular. Plastic surgeons can do amazing things these days . . . Are you listening, Bowser?"

Battle put the bread out and got ham from the refrigerator. Plangman was cracked, he thought. He spread mustard on the bread. "Yes, I'm listening."

"I need to change myself. I'm tired of myself. Do you know I feel I can say anything to you? Anything! I don't even care if you laugh."

"Good!" said Battle.

"I need my chin built up, wouldn't you say? How much money *do* you have, sir?"

He could tell by the sounds from the other room that Plangman was going through his things. He knew Plangman was trying to cover up the sounds of drawers opening by speaking in a loud voice. He poured a glass of milk and put the sandwich together.

"I don't have much money," he called back to Plangman. He stalled. He called in, "Whatever happened to my passport?" None of the letters he had written to Plangman contained the name Bowser or Battle; there had been no return address on them.

"Oh, I have your passport with me, sir."

There was a claw hammer on the window sill. Battle walked across and picked it up. He stuffed it into his back trousers' pocket, pulled down his sweater over it, then picked up the plate with the sandwich on it, and the glass of milk.

From the other room, Plangman said, "But you don't want to go any place, do you?"

"I sort of do," said Raymond Battle, starting into the other room.

NINETEEN

"SLEEPING?" HE said.

"I can't sleep! Ray, do you have a girl down there, is that what it's all about?"

"No, I don't have a girl down here. But my friend got sick all over my rug, dammit. I have a good mind to just take it to the city dump!"

"Is he gone?"

"I'm going to drive him to the bus station. I don't want him to stay over."

"Banjo's been calling and calling," she yawned. "And I've just hung up every time! I can't face telling him we're getting married. You know, he really goes for me, Ray, he . . ."

"Bunny, I can't talk!"

"What's the matter with you anyway, Ray! You don't have to . . ."

"My friend is waiting," he said, looking down at the rug, rolled and tied. "I just called to say I love you and I'll see you tomorrow."

"You don't want me to wait up until you get back?"

"No, it's too late already!"

"Don't snap, Ray!"

"I'm sorry."

"Thank you."

"I'll see you tomorrow."

She said, "Nite! Nite!"

He shut his eyes after he hung up, and gave himself a few slow seconds to go over everything. Then he picked up Plangman's suitcase (the passport was in it; so was all of Plangman's identification now), and the pillow case containing Plangman's clothes, and his own bloody clothing. There was a carton of beer in the pillow case too, which he had taken from the refrigerator. On the Hinkson, a woodsy spot north of Columbia, where the students went for beer parties, it was the custom to bury any fire, and all cans and other refuse after a party. He would empty the

167

beer cans near the ground where he would make the grave,
build a fire and burn the bloody clothing. Just another
party on the Hinkson; a typical time for it too, he would
get there around two-thirty. Over his arm was a clean pair
of trousers, a fresh shirt, and another sweater. He might
need to change his clothes again, if there was blood on him
again, when he finished. He had brought up a shovel from
the basement and placed it just outside the door of 702.
When he was through at the Hinkson, he would drive to the
bus station and check Plangman's suitcase—get it out of the
way until he was sure of how to dispose of it.

He glanced back at the room. The room was clean
enough. At the last minute he had retrieved a tooth from
under the chair, and he flushed it down the toilet. The
hammer was washed and back in its place on the window
sill. He could drag the rug down the hall and out the door
and cram it into the trunk of the car. He was sure he
could manage it. He would back the car to the door; the
street was quiet at this hour. It was time now—and
luck. Luck!

He shut the door behind him and walked out of 702,
down Wentwroth and around the corner where his car was
parked. It was exactly two-fifteen. He put the suitcase and
the laundry bag in the back seat with his change of clothes.
He would have to remember matches—oven matches from
the house. Folder matches were stubborn and could go out . . .
even in the slightest breeze—like that. Matches. He made a
mental note while he unlocked the trunk of his car and moved
the spare tire to the back seat. Plangman had not called his
mother; that was in Battle's favor. He wondered how long
it would be before Plangman was missed. When he was
missed, there would be no reason to connect Battle to the
fact. They would be hunting for him in the East. In a day
or two, Battle would call on Mrs. Plangman, explain that
he was marrying Bunny and accepting a job abroad. He
would help her make arrangements for someone to take his
place at 702.

He started the car and drove up College Avenue to Stil-
son, down Stilson to the cross street connecting with Went-
wroth. It might be months before anyone missed Plangman.
He was a bad correspondent, unless he wanted something;
Mrs. Plangman had complained about that often enough.
He could not feel sorry for Plangman, nor any remorse.
He had been victimized by Plangman for too long. Plang-

man had died as he had lived, trying to horn in where he didn't fit. He was victim, now, of his victim—appropriate.

Battle backed the car into the drive at 702. He got out and went for the shovel, put it in the trunk, and lifted the lid. Then he went down the hall, pushed open his door, and saw Banjo on his knees by the rug.

"Jesus, Ray, what's going on around here? There's blood leaking out of this thing! I just came over because I was worried about Bunny and the kids. Bunny hung up when I called and I was worried. Ray, what the hell's going on?" His face was very white. He stood up and faced Battle, trembling. "I put my car away, and then I got to thinking, and I walked back this way, came down the hall to your place and the door was . . ."

Raymond Battle walked over to him. "I wish you hadn't come," he said, "but here you are." He looked at Banjo's white frightened face, and saw in those weak and shallow features the undoing of all his plans. "Here you are," he said grimly, "and as you say, there's blood leaking out."

"What's up, Ray?" Banjo said in a small voice, so insignificant-sounding you wouldn't think that it even counted at all in the scheme of things, but there you were. "Where's Bun . . ."

Banjo fell across the rug containing Harvey Plangman, at the impact of Raymond Battle's angry fist, hard on his jaw.

He went directly to the car, shut the trunk lid, and started the motor. By five a.m. he had reached St. Louis.

He pulled into a parking lot near the train station. From the suitcase in the back seat, he removed Robert Bowser's passport and Harvey Plangman's wallet. He stuck them in his trousers pocket with his own wallet. The rest he left, and he left the key in the ignition.

He accepted the ticket from the man attending the parking lot. His attitude was one of resignation and resolve. It was a case of simple survival now, no embellishments, no time for plans, no wish to dream, regret, wonder, or hesitate. He walked across to the train station, and into the men's. He paid a dime for a private washroom. Inside, he opened Plangman's wallet, took out fifteen fifty-dollar bills, ten twenties, and five tens. He stuffed them into his trousers. He glanced through the rest of the wallet. There were the same photographs, the letter from Gertrude, a book of matches from a place called Allgauer's, in Chicago, and a folded piece of paper. He unfolded the paper and read it.

    HARVEY PLANGMAN
    Hadden Planner
    Halden Planman
    Hadren Plann
    Hansel Planor
    Harris Plantman   .
    Heath P. Langman. (H. P. Langman)

There was a check mark after Hansel Planor and one after Heath P. Langman.

Under that list was a heading: Vocabulary.

    soigné—painstakingly attended to, well-groomed.
    perjorative—disapproving, deprecating.
    gens du monde—fashionable people of the world;
      society.
    coûte que coûte—cost what it may.

Then three notations at the bottom:

    Royall Lyme Toilet Lotion Supreme (Brooks
      Brothers)
    Jose Cuervo Tequila
    Gold antelope cross-over Hatton Case vest.

Battle ripped up the note and dropped it into the empty wire disposal basket beside the sink. He tossed the wallet on top.

The basket then contained all that was left of Harvey Plangman. Battle looked around for some paper towels to cover the pathetic remainders. The towels were cloth, on a roller. He tore off some toilet tissue from the container and let it fall on Plangman's things. Rest In Peace.

He straightened the collar of his shirt and smoothed down his sweater, brushed off his trousers with his hand. Then he combed his hair and wiped a smudge off his chin with his thumb. The eastbound trains for New York left at the south side of the station; he had checked that upon entering. From the wad of bills in his wallet, he took two tens and a five, and put them in a separate pocket, so there would be no chance of the money spilling out when he bought his ticket. He looked at his reflection once more in the mirror, took a deep breath, and turned to leave. As he pushed out the door, a large man in a heavy blue coat, carrying a suitcase, pushed in. They bumped heads.

"Oh, I'm sorry!" the man said, "I didn't know that..."

Battle felt the sharp edge of pain in his eyelid. He rubbed his eye with his fingers in a quick, automatic, unthinking gesture, and the pain went. He blinked.

"My lens!" he said.

"What? Are you leaving or aren't you?" said the man.

"I'm not. I..." Battle closed the eye he could not see out of, and stood holding the door, squinting down at the floor.

"What's the matter?"

"My lens!" Battle snapped. "You pushed me and I lost my lens!"

"I didn't push you. I pushed the door and you were coming out of it."

Battle got down on his knees, holding the door with his hand. With the palm of his other hand, he felt the floor. The man dropped his suitcase and Battle glared up at him, shouting, "Pick that up! Can't you see I've lost something!"

The man pushed it away with his foot, it scraped along the floor and Battle imagined his lens being ground under it. "Damn you!" Battle said. "Pick it up!"

A third man came over. "What's the matter?"

"Get back!" said Battle. "I've lost my lens. You could be stepping on it right this minute."

The third man held the door. "What's a lens?"

The man in the blue coat said, "That's what I'd like to know." He picked up his suitcase and went off to another wash booth.

Battle said to the third man, "It's a contact lens. It fell out of my eye." He was on all fours now, feeling his way. He said, "I can't see without it. It's very important."

"Here," said the man. He bent over and handed Battle a small pocket flashlight. "How big is the thing?"

"Very tiny. It's right around here someplace, but it could have fallen back inside."

The man stuck a pencil in the door hinge. "I'll help you," he said. "I'll look in here."

"Careful," Battle warned him. "Watch where you step."

The man was behind him, searching near the sink.

"It's very tiny," Battle cautioned him again.

"Did you just leave here? Were you coming out just now?"

"Yes, and that fellow was coming in. We bumped heads and he knocked it out of position. It's right around here."

"The woman just emptied these things," the man said. He was jiggling the wire disposal basket with his hand. "Did you throw this stuff in here?"

Battle stopped feeling the floor. He looked up at the man.

"Did you just throw this stuff in here?" the man said again. He reached down and picked up the wallet. "Empty," he said. "Empty of money but the identification's here."

Battle mumbled. "It's an old wallet."

"You just threw it out with all of your girlfriends' pictures in it?"

"It's none of your business," said Battle.

"Yes, it is," the man said. "You better get up on your feet."

Battle stood. He squinted with his good eye. The man opened his coat enough to show a badge. "Turn around," he said.

Battle turned around. He felt the hand reach in and remove the wallet of Raymond Battle—and next to that, Robert Bowser's passport.

TWENTY

TOGETHER THEY waited at the entranceway of the train station for the squad car. The policeman was talkative, in good spirits as a result of his catch. It was getting light out now; the policeman said St. Louis was prettiest this time of morning.

"My wife and I moved into a new place, and what a view we got," he said. "Of course we're paying for it, a hell of a lot more than I can afford, but we like things nice. We see eye to eye on that. That's why we don't want kids. Can't afford kids and nice things too."

Battle said nothing.

"Smoke Mr.——Battle, Bowser, Plangman——take your pick. Smoke?"

Battle reached for a cigarette from the pack.

"They'll probably taste a little strange to you. They're Turkish Specials. I got so I like them. They're not much more than ordinary cigarettes, and they're something different from what everyone else smokes, you know?"

He lit Battle's cigarette with a silver lighter shaped like a sword, with a monogram down the side.

He said, "Yep! We all wanna be different. Special. That's where the trouble starts in life, I suppose. Take you with them lenses. I'm sorry we never found the other one. But y'know, I probably wouldn't have picked you up tonight, if you weren't wearing them things. What'd you wanna do, beautify yourself?"

"No," said Battle flatly.

"Ha, ah! The gorgeous pickpocket. Ha-ah! Well, that's the way it all starts. We wanna improve ourselves, y'know? Or maybe it's a disguise. Maybe you're really a big crook, head of the Mafia, or something. Ha, ah!" He sucked in on his cigarette and chuckled to himself. "No, nope," he sighed. "I met a few of the big ones in my day. They're another story altogether. You know they get their fingergnails manicured just like dames? Fancy this and fancy that, and some of them smell like dames. Use men's perfume, you know? Now,

173

me, I use a little something after I shave. Dunhill, it's called. Come in bottles shaped like bowling pins. Costs a little more than some stuff, but it's nice to have something that's yours. You use it exclusively, you know? It's exclusive."

"Umm hmm," said Battle. The sky was very pink now, the traces of night gone, and streaks of blue starting to stripe the pink.

The policeman said, "But these big fellows, their stuff smells like what my wife'd wear. I buy her that Chanel No. 5 that they used to give away on the old Stork Club show. That show was years ago on the television. Come from New York, and it showed Sherman Billingsley and his Stork Club, and this Chanel No. 5 my wife wears. Someday I'm going to take her to the Stork Club. Coupla drinks is all. Say we been there. I bet they charge like hell. You ever hear of the place? It's very fancy."

"Yes," Battle said. "I've heard of the place."

"Now, there's where you should pick the pockets, off the people who got something in them, you know? These big fellows with their paws manicured and Chanel No. 5 behind their ears—they can afford the Stork Club and lots better. I met a few of them in my time. I never met one down on all fours in the hopper, though, ha-ah! You meet all kinds in the hopper—cannons, perverts, name it and the hopper's got it, but not the big fellows. Like Costello. He's getting himself shaved some fancy place when he got it, some fancy place in New York. Well, listen, I got to hand it to them. They got a way about them, you know? They know exactly what they want, and that's what they want. Shoes, hats, ties, they know exactly what they want and it's exclusive. They just don't go about getting it very honestly, ha-ah!"

Battle shifted his weight from one foot to the other and sighed.

"You're not much of a talker, are you?" the policeman said.

"No, I'm not."

"Well, I wouldn't be if I was in your shoes either. Say, speaking of shoes, did you see the shoes on that fellow bumped into you?"

"No, I didn't."

"They were those fancy space shoes, you know? I noticed that fellow the minute he came in the hopper. Very snazzy guy. I don't want to break your heart or anything, but I was on my way out of the hopper when he came in. I stuck around because of him. It wasn't just the shoes. It was the coat. Did you notice the coat?"

"No, I didn't notice the coat," Battle said. The squad car came around the corner then; two uniformed policemen were in the front seat.

"Well, here's the old paddy wagon," said the policeman. "Yeah, that was a coat! Kind I'd like myself." He ground out his cigarette with his shoe. I never saw one of them coats in blue," he said. "I suppose they cost a little more, but what the hell! It's different. I always notice things like that. Those shoes and that coat."

He took Battle's arm and led him toward the squad car.

"It was a Loden coat," he said. "I didn't know you could get a blue Loden coat."

One of the uniformed policemen hung his head out the window and said, "Well, now, if it isn't St. Louis' Aristocrat of Cops! No doubt that's the Duke of Windsor with you, and you both want to be returned to your castles. Or would it be the Count of Everything Exclusive who's accompanying you this fine morning?"

The policeman holding onto Battle snickered. "Ride me all you want, wise guy," he said. "Just don't try to bum one of my Turkish Specials offa me!"

THE END